Praise for ALL GROWN UP

A National Bestseller

"[I read] *All Grown Up* attentively, in a single gulp . . . Attenberg, with her wry sense of humor, manages to entertain and move us . . . Whatever Andrea's objectives are, we're rooting for her."　　　　　　**—New York Times Book Review**

"Jami Attenberg's acerbic, astute *All Grown Up* is an exploration of the singular challenges of modern womanhood, and it's often a hilarious one . . . [An] exquisitely of-the-moment novel."　　　　　　**—O, The Oprah Magazine**

"Hilarious, courageous and mesmerizing from page one, *All Grown Up* is a little gem that packs a devastating wallop. It's that rare book I'm dying to give all my friends so we can discuss it deep into the night. I'm in awe of Jami Attenberg."
　　—Maria Semple, author of *Where'd You Go, Bernadette?*

"Thank you, Jami Attenberg, for pushing back against society's assumptions about what is allowed to matter in our lives. For giving us a different kind of narrative. *All Grown Up* is not all fluffy and lovely. It turns out that we have other stories—we single people. We human beings."
　　　　　　　　　　　　　　　　　　—Bustle

"This is a novel about how to step up when your smug married friend suddenly gets divorced, or when your annoying mum really needs you; about 'being there' for people when you don't even know where 'there' is. It has hope, in spades."   —*Guardian*

"Jami Attenberg deftly travels inside the head of a thirty-nine-year-old woman who has no interest in doing what she's supposed to do and follows her heart instead of her mind—a story that's sexy, charming, and impossible to put down."   —*Newsweek*

"Deeply enjoyable."   —*Elle*

"Jami Attenberg's sharply drawn protagonist, Andrea, has such a riveting, propulsive voice that *All Grown Up* is hard to put down, but I urge you to resist reading it in one sitting. Both the prose and the author's knowing excavation of one woman's desires, compromises, strengths, and fears deserve closer attention. Like Andrea herself, this novel is beautiful and brutal, intelligent and funny, frank and sexy."
—*Cynthia D'Aprix Sweeney*,
New York Times best-selling author of *The Nest*

"Attenberg knows how to make a reader laugh and *feel*. This novel takes a hard look at what it means to be a woman living on her own terms."   —*Martha Stewart Living*

"Attenberg is one of our finest contemporary storytellers, and here, with her trademark clever, witty voice, she tackles the age-old question plaguing people of all ages: When do we know if we're actually all grown up?" —*Nylon*

"Smart, heartfelt, and really freakin' funny." —**Elle.com**

"Jami Attenberg's Andrea is the most addicting female protagonist voice I have read in years, with her cutting observations on human relationships. This witty journey through a mess of men, female friendships, family, and boozy urban existence positions the single girl not as object to be fixed but as contemporary sage and seer: the ultimate witness of truth in love today." —*Melissa Broder,*
author of *So Sad Today*

"Attenberg's fifth novel is her best yet. It's a super-smart, often extremely funny, sometimes heartbreaking portrait of a thirty-nine-year-old, single, child-free heroine in New York City who's taking her very best shot at living life on her own terms . . . As angry, sad, and raw as it is astute, hilarious, and hopeful, *All Grown Up* puts other novels in this vein to shame." —*Observer*

"Attenberg's latest takes on the ridiculous standards we set for ourselves, all with humor and aching relatability." —*PureWow*

"Amidst the gems of mordant wit, *All Grown Up* plumbs deeper, darker veins: the ready ease with which sex (and drugs and alcohol) can become coping mechanisms, the specter of being stuck forever as everyone else moves on, 'architecting new lives.' Do yourself a favor and buy this book."   —*Buzzfeed Books*

"Told in smart and funny vignettes, *All Grown Up* is an examination of what it means to be a woman and a grown-up in today's times. This deceptively short novel will stay with you long after finishing the last page."   —*PopSugar*

"Jami Attenberg has written her frankest, funniest, and most riveting and heartbreaking book yet. In Andrea, she has created a character women will be talking about for years; she has opened the door for us to see ourselves in literature in a new way, writing with skill and fearlessness few others can match."   —**Emily Gould,** author of *Friendship*

"With a flair for understatement and crack timing, she makes Andrea Bern immensely flawed but highly resilient and self-aware, capable of reflecting on the lack of ballast in her life without drowning in clichés or Issues. It's essential to the story that Andrea is unreservedly single; what makes it so good is that she's absolutely singular."   —*Vulture*

"With a satirical voice and astounding pathos, Attenberg's latest protagonist draws readers into the enthralling and thought-provoking world she inhabits, against the backdrop of an important social conversation about contemporary gender roles." —*Harper's Bazaar*

"Wise and witty." —*People,* The Best New Books

"Deeply perceptive and dryly hilarious, Attenberg's latest novel follows Andrea Bern: on the cusp of forty, single, child-free by choice, and reasonably content, she's living a life that still, even now, bucks societal conventions . . . Structured as a series of addictive vignettes—they fly by if you let them, though they deserve to be savored—the novel is a study not only of Andrea, but of her entire ecosystem . . . Wry, sharp, and profoundly kind; a necessary pleasure."
—*Kirkus Reviews,* starred review

"Jami Attenberg's *All Grown Up* is one part Denis Johnson, one part Grace Paley, but all her. Every sentence pulls taut and glows—electric, gossipy, searing fun that is also a map to how to be more human."
—**Alexander Chee,** author of *The Queen of the Night*

"Funny, insightful." —*Dallas Morning News*

"Addicting and incredibly refreshing . . . Attenberg brings the often upsetting, often comedic realities of life across in poignant, astute vignettes that will live in the reader's heart for a long, long time." —*Travel + Leisure*

"*All Grown Up* [is] a smart, funny/sad, and unflinchingly honest novel about a single New Yorker . . . In sparkling prose, [Attenberg] brings this wonderful character so fully to life that after the book ended, I found myself wishing Andrea well, as if she were a good friend, and wondering what she would do next."
—*Milwaukee Journal Sentinel*

"What a voice. Honest and hilarious, unflinching and un-apologetic, Jami Attenberg writes what it is to be single, sexual, and child-free by choice. I read the first page of *All Grown Up* and knew the novelist was going to outdo herself. I am happy to report that she most certainly did."
—**Helen Ellis,** author of *American Housewife*

"Is all life junk—sparkly and seductive and devastat-ing—just waiting to be told correctly by someone who will hold our hand and walk with us awhile, confirming that what we're living is true? This is a good proud urban book, a sad and specific blast for the fearless to read. Thank you, Jami."
—**Eileen Myles,** author of *Chelsea Girls*

"Andrea, thirty-nine, is totally single. No kids, no men, nothing keeping her from living her life to its full potential, which she does. Until her niece is born with a tragic illness, and Andrea's whole family is forced to confront their values, their lifestyles, and their choices. Told in vignettes, *All Grown Up* asks what happens after you've got the whole 'adult' thing under control."

—*Glamour,* Best Books to Read in 2017

"*All Grown Up* is one of those rare books—even the greatest writers often only get one or two in their careers—in which an author's unique sensibility meets with the story she was born to tell. This fractured, soulful portrait of a determinedly independent woman—a woman whose radical independence often puts her at odds with a misunderstanding society—is vital reading for women and men alike."

—**Stefan Merrill Block,** author of
The Story of Forgetting and *The Storm at the Door*

"Andrea's story is stinging, sweet, and remarkably fleshed out in relatively few pages. Attenberg follows her best-selling family novel, *The Middlesteins,* with a creative, vivid tableau of one woman's whole life, which almost can't help but be a comment on all the things women ought to be and to want, which Attenberg conveys with immense, aching charm." —*Booklist,* starred review

ALL GROWN UP

ALL GROWN UP

JAMI ATTENBERG

Mariner Books
Houghton Mifflin Harcourt
Boston   New York

First Mariner Books edition 2018

Copyright © 2017 by Jami Attenberg

Reading Group Guide © 2017 by Houghton Mifflin Harcourt
Publishing Company

Interview with Edan Lepucki first appeared online at *The Millions*.

hmhco.com

Library of Congress Cataloging-in-Publication Data is available.
ISBN 978-0-544-82424-9 (hardcover)
ISBN 978-1-328-91532-0 (paperback)
ISBN 978-0-544-82426-3 (ebook)

Book design by Greta D. Sibley

Printed in the United States of America
DOC 10 9 8 7 6 5 4 3 2 1

ALL GROWN UP

The Apartment

You're in art school, you hate it, you drop out, you move to New York City. For most people, moving to New York City is a gesture of ambition. But for you, it signifies failure, because you grew up there, so it just means you're moving back home after you couldn't make it in the world. Spiritually, it's a reverse commute.

For a while you live downtown with your brother and his girlfriend, in a small spare room, your bed jammed between shoe racks and a few of your brother's guitars in cases plus a wall of books from his girlfriend's undergraduate days at Brown. You get a job, via same girlfriend. You don't hate the job and you don't love the job, but you can't sniff at a hard day's work because you are no better than anyone else, and, in some ways, you are much, much worse. You acknowledge your privilege, and you get to work.

You start making money. You find a small, dusty, crumbling loft in a shitty waterfront neighborhood in Brooklyn. It has one floor-to-ceiling window, a tiny Empire State Building in the distance framed beautifully within it. Now you are home. Everyone in your life breathes easier. She's safe now, they all think. At no point does anyone say to you, "So you've stopped making art?" It is because they don't want to know the answer or they don't care or they are scared to ask you because you scare them. Whatever the case, everyone is complicit in this, this new, non-art-making phase of your life. Even though it was the thing you loved most in the world.

But you have a little secret: while you are not making Art anymore you are at least drawing every day. To tell anyone about this would be admitting there is a hole in your life, and you'd rather not say that out loud, except in therapy. But there you are, once a day, drawing the same thing over and over: that goddamned Empire State Building. You get up every morning (or afternoon, on the weekends, depending on the hangover), have a cup of coffee, sit at the card table near the window, and draw it, usually in pencil. If you have time, you'll ink it. Sometimes, if you are running late for work, you do it at night instead, and then you add color to the sketches, to reflect the building's ever-changing lights. Sometimes you draw just the building and sometimes you draw the buildings around it and sometimes you draw the sky and sometimes you draw the bridge in the foreground and sometimes you draw the East River and sometimes you draw the window frame around the whole scene. You have sketchbooks full of these drawings. You could draw the same thing forever, you realize. *No man ever steps in the same river twice, for it's not the same river, and he's not the same man* is a thing you read once. The Empire State Building is your river. And you don't have to leave your apartment to step in it. Art feels safe for you again, even though you know you are not getting any better at it, that the work you are making could be sold to tourists on a sidewalk outside of Central Park on a sunny Saturday and that's about it. There's no challenge to it, no message, just your view, on repeat. But this is all you can do, this is all you have to offer, and it is just enough to make you feel special.

You do this for six years. Brooklyn apartment in a changing neighborhood, why move when the rent is so cheap? Mediocre but well-paying job at which you excel; you receive a few small promotions. Volunteer work here and there. You march where your activist mother tells you to march. Pointless sketchbooks pile up on the bottom row of a bookshelf. Barely scratching a feverish itch. You also drink plenty and for a long time use, too, coke and ecstasy mainly, although sometimes pills to bring you down at the end of the night. Another way to scratch the itch. There are men also, in your bed, in your world, foggily, but you are less interested in them than in muffling the voice in your head that says you are doing absolutely nothing with your life, that you are a child, that the accoutrements of adulthood are bullshit, they don't mean a goddamn thing, and you are trapped between one place and another and you always will be unless something forces you to change. And also, you miss making art.

Other people you know seem to change quite easily. They have no problem at all with succeeding at their careers and buying apartments and moving to other cities and falling in love and getting married and hyphenating their names and adopting rescue cats and, finally, having children, and then documenting all of this meticulously on the internet. Really, it appears to be effortless on their part. Their lives are constructed like buildings, each precious but totally unsurprising block stacked before your eyes.

Your favorite thing is when a friend asks to meet you for a drink, a friend you have had a million drinks with in your life, and then, when you get to the bar, your friend stares at the menu and orders nothing, and you are forced to say, "Aren't you drinking?" and she says, "I wish," and she pauses dramatically and you know exactly what's coming next: she's about to tell you she's pregnant. And there is this subtext that you are lucky because you can still drink, and she's unlucky because she can't drink, she has this dumb baby in her. What a stupid fucking baby. In her.

Eventually your brother and his wife get pregnant, and you can't hate on that because it's family, and also they've always been incredibly kind to you, your brother and you particularly bonded because of your father's young demise, an overdose. You throw a baby shower, at which you drink too many mimosas and cry in the bathroom, but you are pretty sure no one notices. It's not that you want a baby, or want to get married, or any of it. It's not your bag. You just feel tired for some reason. Tired of the world. Tired of trying to fit in where you don't. You go home that night and draw the Empire State Building and you feel hopeful doing this thing you love to do, so hopeful you look up online what tonight's colors mean—the lights are green and blue—and find out it's in honor of National Eating Disorders Day and you get depressed all over again even though you've never had an eating disorder in your life.

Nine months come and go, a baby could be born at any minute. You call your brother to find out when exactly, but they've been using a hippie-dippie midwife and he says, "We don't know yet. Could be another week." You are suddenly aswirl with enthusiasm. It's going to be a girl. "Call me whenever you hear anything, anything at all," you tell him. Then you have three intensely dull, soul-deadening afternoon meetings in a row and after that you are moved to a new cube, which you must share with a freshly hired coworker who is thirteen years younger than you and is hilarious and loud and pretty and is probably making half of what you make but still spends it all on tight dresses. It is a Friday. You go out for drinks in your neighborhood. You get lit. Then you call your dealer, whom you haven't called in a few years. You can't believe the number still works. He says, "It's been a while since we last met." You say, "I've been busy," as if you need to justify why you're not doing drugs anymore. You don't buy that much, just enough, but then you meet a man at the bar—you both pretend you've met before although you haven't, but it just feels safer that way for some reason—and he has more than enough for the two of you. Then you go home together, to your place, to tiny Manhattan in the window, to the piles of sketchbooks, and the two of you proceed to do all the drugs. This goes on for hours. There's a little bit of sex involved but neither one of you is that interested in each other. Drug buddies, that's about it. You can't even get it up to get it up. Eventually he leaves, and you turn off your phone and go to sleep. You wake up on Sunday night. You turn on your phone. There are eight messages from your brother and your mother. You have missed your niece being born.

You don't do any drugs after that, ever again. No rehab necessary. You start to see the world with fresh eyes. But the world looks the same. Job, apartment, friends, family, view. For a few weeks it seems like they might try to give you an enormous promotion at work, but then you realize you'll have more responsibility so you wiggle your way out of it. This promotion would mean you're staying there for a while. You lie to yourself: I should keep my options open. You never know what could happen.

Still you draw. This is the best part of your day. This is your purest moment. This is when the breath leaves your body and you feel like you are hovering slightly above the ground. On New Year's, that day of fresh starts, you allow yourself to flip through some of the old sketchbooks. You recognize you have gotten better. You are not *not* talented. That is a thing that fills you up. You sit with it. You sit with yourself. You allow yourself that pleasure of liking yourself. What if this is enough?

A week later, you are leaving your apartment building and you notice a fence around the lot across the street. There is a sign up, a construction permit. A ten-story condo building. Starts in a month. You live on the fifth floor. This building will block your view, no question. For a second you wonder if this is a joke. You look behind you to see if there's a camera filming you, waiting for your reaction, but no, it's real, your life is about to change. At last, something surprises you.

It takes a year for the building to go up, and you watch the construction every day. Brick by brick. You can't tell when it will be finished exactly, when you'll finally lose the view, but you decide to throw one last party to signify the end. You invite everyone you know and you even allow children to come. Your friends toast the Empire State Building, and you. "It was a good view," says one of your old work friends, her fiancé in tow. "It wasn't a million-dollar view," you say, "but it was worth fifteen hundred a month." "You have such a good deal," says her fiancé. "You can't move, even without the view. You can never leave this apartment," he says and shakes your shoulders.

The day the final brick is cemented and your view is officially gone, you buy a bottle of wine and order a pizza and sit at your table. You stare at air and nothing and brick. The thing that made you special is gone. You will never have that view back, nor that time. And all you have to show for it are these sketchbooks, which are useless anyway. You think about burning them, but what good would that do? And they're the only things that prove you existed on this earth. You realize all along you were just trying to prove to yourself you were still alive. *But if I don't have this, am I dead?* Surely not. Please, no. You take a bite of your pizza and a sip of your wine and ask yourself the question you're finally ready to ask: What next?

ANDREA

A book is published. It's a book about being single, written by an extremely attractive woman who is now married, and it is a critical yet wistful remembrance of her uncoupled days. I have no interest in reading this book. I am already single. I have been single a long time. There is nothing this book can teach me about being single that I don't already know.

Regardless, everyone I know tells me about this book. They are like carrier pigeons, fluttering messages, doing the bidding of a wicked media maestro on a rooftop in midtown Manhattan. Nothing will stop them from reaching their destination, me, their presumed target demographic.

My coworker Nina, the bangles on her wrist clinking, hands me her copy when she's finished with it, even though I have never expressed an interest in reading it, let alone discussed it with her. She is newly single, and she is twenty-four. A woman who was not newly single, and also not twenty-four, would know better than to hand this book to another single woman.

My mother orders a copy for me online and it shows up one day, a surprise in the mail, without a note or a name attached, and it takes me a week to figure out who sent it to me. The whole time I am thinking: A ghost sent me this book. A ghost wants me to think about being single.

Finally my mother confesses she sent it. (She does not see it as a confession, of course. I am the only one who sees it that way.) "Did you get the book?" she asks. "Oh, *you* sent the book," I say. "Mom, why would you send a book like that to me?" "I thought it would be helpful," she says.

My sister-in-law, who lives in the hinterlands of New Hampshire and who has dedicated her life to taking care of her dying child, my niece, and spends her days contemplating mortality, mentions this book to me on the phone during my weekly Sunday phone call to her home. "Have you heard about this book?" she says. "Yes," I say. "I have heard about the book."

Old college friends post links to reviews of it on my Facebook wall and say things like, "Sounds like something you'd like," or "This reminded me of you." I think, Am I supposed to like this? I don't, in fact, like it. I dislike it. Where is my dislike button? Where do I click to scream?

I go to my therapist and say, "Why is being single the only thing people think of when they think of me? I'm other things, too."

And this delights her, this old, wry, wrinkled, brainy bitch. This feels like a breakthrough, at the very least a valuable exercise, a teachable moment. Something. This is a change in our conversation. An assertion is being made, a thesis statement about my life, finally. "Tell me who you are, then," she says. "What other statements are true?"

"Well, I'm a woman," I say.

"Good, yes."

"I work in advertising as a designer."

"Yes."

"I'm technically a Jew."

"OK."

"I'm a New Yorker."

I start to feel unsettled. Surely I am more than that.

"I'm a friend," I say. "I'm a daughter, I'm a sister, I'm an aunt." Those things feel farther away lately, but they exist as part of my identity.

In my head I think:

I'm alone.

I'm a drinker.

I'm a former artist.

I'm a shrieker in bed.

I'm the captain of the sinking ship that is my flesh.

To my therapist I say, "I'm a brunette."

I go out on a date with a man I meet online and it does not go well. Although there's a certain pleasure I take in not being the one who drinks too much on the date, it's only momentary, because I still have to contend with a drunk, I still have to spend time with this man, monitor whether he'll be hostile or joyful. I have to step outside myself. This is not a date; this is an audition for a play about a terrible date.

He's two bourbons in by the time I arrive, and I'm patient but then sour about it when I feel that he's touching me too much. He's too familiar, too presumptuous, and also he's wearing a turtleneck and he does not have the right head for a turtleneck, or maybe it's just his chin, or his mouth, I don't even know, I mean I just *can't* with that turtleneck. And then, as we part ways, he asks me if I've read it, read the book. I say, "No, have you?" And he says, "No, I don't read a lot," and I think, *Quelle surprise*. And then he adds, "But I can tell it's totally about you." And I say, "You're single too, why isn't it about *you*?" And he says, "Oh, this? This is just temporary for me."

The permanence of my impermanence. I stand in possession of it. I stand before him at the entrance to a subway station, in possession of nothing but myself. Myself is everything, I want to tell him. But to him it is nothing, because that's how he feels about himself right now. He is alone, and so he is nothing. How do I explain to him that what applies to him does not apply to me? His context is not my context. How do you blow up the bus you've been forced to ride your entire life? It wasn't your fault there were no other means of transportation available.

"You should read it," he says, and I swat him in the arm with my purse as if I have been assaulted and want him to leave me alone. I exit the scene, audition over, and he yells after me his final line: "Hey, what was that for?" If he called me a bitch, I can't recall hearing it now. It was probably under his breath. A last-minute improvisation.

I never read the book. I leave it in the laundry room of my apartment building, and it is gone the next time I return. My mother doesn't ask about it again. Her assessment of my burdens is ever-changing. Singleness forgotten for the moment.

Let's forget it, shall we? Can we all just talk about something else, please?

INDIGO GETS
MARRIED

I fly to Seattle, by myself, to go to my friend Indigo's wedding. She was one of the first work friends I made when I started in advertising, and we drank together at happy hour events in midtown practically every Thursday night for several years, and even took a few vacations together, just weekends away, but still. Her mother is Trinidadian and her father is white and everywhere I went with her, men would tell her she was "exotic," and she would always reply, "I am not a bird or a flower, I am a human being." She eventually quit her job to become a yoga instructor, but she is marrying a rich man, so she works only part-time. Nevertheless, they throw a hippie wedding, or at least it has the trappings of one. They are both barefoot. There are wildflowers everywhere. Her dress appears to be in tatters. We

are in someone's backyard, although this particular backyard has a view of Puget Sound.

I sit at the singles table under a nest of twinkling lights
and grape leaves. There are four other single women at the
table: two of them are lesbians, who are best friends with
each other and seem invested in gossiping about everyone
they went to college with; one of them is a retired nun,
whose story remains mysterious throughout the night; and
the fourth woman is Karen, a real career gal. I say this not to
make fun of her but because she described herself as such,
which means it is doubly true. There are two gay men at
the table, who used to date and are using the evening as
an opportunity to hash out a few things, and there are two
straight men: a newly divorced uncle of the groom named
Warren, and a tall, broad, masculine man named Kurt, who
works at the corporate headquarters of the Seattle Mariners.

I watch Karen get toasted quickly on Sancerre, and
Kurt joins her, but he's drinking Scotch. They flirt heavily,
shamelessly, nearly professionally, and it feels like we are no
longer at a wedding but instead are at a bar, and there is a
basket of popcorn in front of them and a sports show playing noiselessly on a television set and a jukebox that keeps
igniting itself every fifteen minutes with a bouncy, Auto-
Tuned pop song. Warren and I sit back and watch them flirt,
our own kind of flirtation. It is like we are on a double date
with them, only we hate them.

"Get a real eyeful," I say to Warren. "This is what you have to look forward to now."

Warren laughs at me. He is in his early fifties and has a smooth, calm demeanor, and he has all of his hair, graying at the temples, and he is rich like his nephew who is marrying my friend Indigo. He tells me he just joined a hiking club. "I used to do it with my wife, and then I was doing it by myself, but I think I'd like to do it with other people sometimes," he says. His arms are tanned and lean. He also tells me he got a dog six months ago, and they go to the park every morning. Just having that dog waiting for him when he gets home is helping him get through this trying time. "I'm glad you got a dog," I say.

We eat oysters, harvested that morning, shucked before serving, an inch deep in their shells. We drink champagne, the good stuff, real, from France, and there is a toast and another and another. Kurt has loosened his tie and put his arm around Karen. He kisses her on the cheek, they whisper in each other's ear. They are plotting. The sun sets behind the Olympics and we are all dazzled. "I've never seen anything like it," I say. I don't leave New York City a lot. "I see it every day and I never tire of it," says Warren.

Kurt and Karen announce they have decided to pretend they are a couple for the rest of the night. Wouldn't that be a hoot? If they pretend they knew each other already, that they've been dating for six months, and that they had shown up together, on a big romantic date. "We met when we were bowling," says Kurt. "No, kayaking," says Karen. "Kayaking, right," says Kurt. "He just had dinner with my mother last weekend for the first time and she loved him," says Karen. "And I loved her. How could I not be charmed by that woman?" says Kurt. Karen is gleeful. "We weren't even supposed to be at this table," she says. "They ran out of room. It was a mistake." The retired nun looks at them blankly. "Why weren't you supposed to be at this table?" "Because we're not single," says Karen. "We're together. We're a couple." "I don't get it," says the nun. "Don't bother trying," I say, and I pat the nun on the hand.

Post-toasts, Karen and Kurt work the room, arms around each other, pretending they're in love. Kurt introduces Karen as his "S.O." to someone. "What's an S.O.?" Warren asks me. "Significant other," I say. Warren sighs deeply and squeezes the edge of the table with his hands. "Oh Warren," I say. "I really did not think going to this would be so hard," he says. "It's only hard if you make it hard," I say. "Come on, let's dance." I am being impulsive here. I don't like dancing. But I could tell Warren would be good on his feet. He's a steady man. He could lead me.

We slow-dance to a cover of Dylan's "Like a Rolling Stone." Whenever the band's lead singer crows, "How does it feel?" the whole crowd sings along with him. Across the dance floor Karen and Kurt are screaming it in each other's face. Indigo and her new husband, Todd, dance over to us. Indigo is stunning, and I tell her so and we hug and dance.

"Is this the best party on the planet?" she says. "It's epic," I say. "Stratospheric." "Did you get enough champagne?" she says. "Everything is perfect," I say. "I'm glad you're dancing with Warren," she says. "I thought you'd get along." "Why did you think that?" I say. "You do so well with wounded men," she says. She leans in close. "You are kinder than you know," she says. Todd grabs her and they dance away before I have a chance to insist that she's wrong. I watch the bride in shredded silk, her ring bigger than all the stars in the sky.

Later, Warren and I sit back at the table alone, our feet splayed on chairs. There are hot fudge sundaes in front of us. I ask him for his cherry and he gives it to me and I greedily eat it. He has been telling me about one of the three companies he owns. Karen and Kurt stumble in front of us. She is holding a bottle of champagne. It is her bottle, and I would like to see anyone try to take it from her.

"How did it go?" I ask. "Did everyone buy it?" "We got busted a few times," admits Kurt. "But it was fun!" says Karen. "Wasn't it fun?" Kurt nods. Kurt seems like he's ready to come back down to earth. "And now we're going back to the hotel," says Karen. "Me and Carl." "It's Kurt," says Kurt. His face darkens. "What?" she says. "My name is Kurt, not Carl." "I meant Kurt," she says. "Oh my god. I'm sorry. You know I know your name, right?" We wait and watch, Warren and I. Kurt and Karen leave together.

"What would you do if you were Kurt?" I say to Warren. "I would take that girl back to her hotel and tuck her in bed and then go back to my own room and jerk off," he says. "Odds are she passes out before anything gets too serious," I say. "And anyway, what if it does?" "I'm old-fashioned, I guess," says Warren. "Are you?" I say. "You're not *old*, though. If that's the way you're feeling. Because you're not." I put my hand on his arm and I am certain my smile is electric. I am thinking about the notion of kindness. I stroke his arm. The night is cool. The band announces it's the last song. He says, "I had a good time with you." I say, "I did, too. We could just continue this. It can be easy and fun. You can come back with me, or I can come with you." I'm still stroking his arm. "I promise you I'm not drunk."

He says, "I know I'm probably a fool for not taking you up on this offer, a lovely young woman like you, but it's just not what I do, not how I am. I'm not saying you're wrong for being how you are, although I can't say it's right either. I can't say any of what I've seen tonight is right." I pull my hand back.

He says, "I was with her for twenty-nine years. We got married right after college. This was the person I was going to die with. I never worried about dating or casual sex or any of that. I don't know how you all do it. I don't know how I'm going to do it. Aren't you lonely?" I say, "Warren, please stop being terrible." He says, "I'm sorry." He pauses, and then his voice grows louder. "No, I'm not sorry. You wanted to have sex with me. And you just met me. You've only known me for three hours." I say, "Warren, I'm sorry. I was wrong after all. You are, in fact, old."

I leave. I have tears in my eyes. Indigo sees me on the way out of the party. "It was such a beautiful night," I say as I wipe my eyes. "I got caught up in the moment. I'm so happy for you." We hug and then I hop into a van that is waiting out front to take me to the hotel. Karen and Kurt are in the van, and when I get in, they stop making out. "You can do better than this," I tell them, but I'm not sure which of them I am speaking to when I say it.

CHARLOTTE

2003, I move into an apartment, one with a tiny view of the Empire State Building, and I can barely get enough money together for the broker's fee and the security deposit and the first and last month's rent, but I do it, and it's a triumph. I can't afford furniture, though. I have a mattress and a small kitchen table that is basically a card table and two chairs and that's it. I end up dumpster-diving in the neighborhood. Two blocks away, outside a senior citizens' home, I find a decent bookshelf, real wood, no nicks. Briefly, I imagine death on it, a resident passing away in the night, her children picking over the china, the jewelry, the sepia-toned family photo albums. *Does anyone want this bookshelf?* No. I hoist it on my back and head home with it, stopping every thirty seconds to rest. It's tall, this bookshelf, and it almost hits the ceiling of my apartment. I dust it, and then

I paint it white while standing on a stepladder. When I'm done, I wipe my hands on my jeans and smile. Overnight the bookshelf dries. I move it against the back wall of the apartment, and I put all my art books in there, organized by color. Then I invite my mother over to see my new place.

The first thing she notices when she walks in is the bookshelf, bright white, and she asks me where I got it. I tell her the truth. "It looks nice," she says. "I just need to do that ten more times and then I'll have a whole apartmentful of furniture," I say, and then I regret it, because I don't want my mother to feel bad that I live that way, even though we've always lived that way, on the edge of broke. She sits down at the kitchen table. I pour some wine into a jelly jar and slide it toward her. For a few minutes she riffs on being alone, missing my father. My mother has been a widow for fifteen years, but she still likes to moan about it whenever her love life gets a little dull. Before she leaves she says, "I can give you furniture," and I say, "Mom, it's fine," and she says, "No, really, I have a few pieces for you," and I don't even know what she's talking about, a few pieces, she's got nothing to spare in her life, and I say no again, and then she gets a little hostile about it and says, "I can give my daughter furniture for her new home if I want to," and finally I agree, and she says she'll send a guy over with it. After she's gone, I drink the rest of the bottle of wine by myself.

A few days later a man shows up with a van. I venture out to the street to see if I can help him carry anything. He's wiry and all jazzed up, with this lean, electric, weird energy. His hair is in tight little curls. He introduces himself as Alonzo. "I'm a friend of your mother's," he says. I ask no questions. My mother has had a lot of friends in her life. She's been a political activist for more than thirty years, involved with every possible shade of leftist organization. We had people coming in and out of our house all the time. Someone helping her out could mean anything. Friendship was fluid.

A woman exits the passenger's side. She's a healthy, big blonde, probably twice the size of the man, both taller than him and wider. "This is my girl visiting from Virginia," he says. She waves at me. He does not mention her name. He opens the back of the van. There's a lamp in there, a small end table, another bookshelf, nothing too impressive, but also a lounge chair with an ottoman, actually gorgeous, black leather with a wood base, an Eames, or a good knock-off, anyway. I haven't been home in a while, but I'm pretty sure my mother just gave me half her living room.

Alonzo and the woman move all of the furniture except for the lamp, which I carry myself. The woman seems to shoulder most of the weight of the furniture while Alonzo quietly directs her. When they're finished, she says to me, "If y'all ever want to sell this chair, let me know. I love it. This is just my kind of chair." There's a genuine hunger in her voice. *This thing would make me happy; this object would please me.* How lucky she is to know what satisfies her. I nearly give it to her then, but I'm too strapped; I need it for myself.

Instead I scrounge in my purse for a tip but Alonzo waves me off. "Your mother took care of everything," he says. He hands me his business card, which has a bunch of job titles on it. He's a carpenter, a DJ, and a motivational speaker. He also does bodywork. "You call me if you ever need anything," he says. "I do it all." I feel like he has everything figured out. I put his business card in my kitchen drawer: my first business card in my new home.

The next week my mother comes to see how her furniture looks in my apartment, and she asks about Alonzo, but really it seems like she's asking about his girlfriend. "Did he take care of you? With that girl of his?" she says. "Who is he to you?" I say. "He's just a friend. He likes to help people. It's what he does," she says. "I don't know anyone like that," I say. "Well, then," she says, "you're hanging out with the wrong kind of people."

Three years pass. I'm nearly thirty-two years old. My mother gets a new boyfriend, and eventually they break up because she finds out he has another girlfriend in Miami, and she says, "That's it. I'm done. That was the last one." During that time my brother gets married to a wonderful woman, and she looks like a princess at the wedding, and it makes me believe in the possibility of love. Even if it doesn't exist for me, it could exist for someone else, and I take comfort in that. I sleep with one of my brother's friends at the wedding and he sneaks out early in the morning without saying goodbye and we never see each other again, until I happen upon his picture in the wedding announcements section of the paper a few years later and I think, Good for you, but also, Fuck you—even though I am not entitled to the feeling at all.

Also during those three years I get two raises at work. Eventually I'm able to pay off the debt from the graduate program I never completed. After that, I buy proper wine-glasses and new bookshelves and a kitchen table, but I keep the lounge chair and the ottoman because I like them. New furniture feels grown up. Also I mostly stop doing drugs, which feels extra grown up. Not in any twelve-step kind of way. I simply couldn't take the hangovers anymore.

But one night I do some coke at a stupid birthday party for one of my old drug friends. I walk into the apartment and everyone's high already and I smell it and I see it on their faces and I want it too because this is the land of no re-percussions, this community, this group of people, this loft in the nethers of Bushwick. I don't even do that much, and I leave before midnight and things can get too dangerous, but then I'm up, I'm fucked. I take a Valium to bring myself down, but it doesn't work—or it works, but it works against me, and I'm racked with terrible sleep. I have a nightmare right before I wake. I'll spare you the specific plot because listening to other people's dreams is boring, but my dead fa-ther was in it. I hadn't thought about him in a while, had actually been actively rejecting thoughts about him for no apparent reason, although if I really pushed myself into a deep kind of consideration about the matter it might have had something to do with a sense of failure and discontentment with my own existence and my fear of mapping that to his personal trajectory, but that's just a guess! An uneducated, bitter, depressed guess. Anyway, there he is, not being particularly threatening or anything, but definitely not friendly either. He's sort of this light blue color, and he's sitting in the recliner with his legs stretched out on the ottoman, a dream, a nightmare, a ghost, all at once.

It scares the shit out of me. I wake up immediately and focus on the room, looking for reality, a steadiness, a center. I stare at the recliner. It's then that I realize that this is the chair where my father overdosed. It was his favorite place to sit, after all. He nodded off there frequently. He died in our living room while I was at school. He was listening to jazz; my mother had mentioned that much. She had never specifically stated where he died. But of course it was in this chair. And now, in my own home, I had napped on that chair. Flipped through the Sunday paper while lounging on it. A few times I had sex on it, not intercourse sex, but oral sex, both given and received. Sex on my father's death chair. Cool gift, Mom.

I call my mother to confirm the truth. She doesn't answer. I leave her a message. For weeks she doesn't return my call, and when she does, I'm on the train to work, which means I can't actually pick up, which means she gets to leave a message. All she says is "Honey, if you don't want the chair then just throw it out."

I call my brother. "Mom gave me the chair Dad died in," I tell him. "And you took it? She tried to give it to me, too," he says. "Well, I didn't know what it was," I say. "I guess I blocked it out." That is a thing I've been known to do, and my brother doesn't argue the point. "I've had nightmares about it," he says. "Just toss it." "Like in the garbage?" I say. "Andrea, just throw it away," he says.

But I understood why my mother held on to it for so long, and also why she felt like she had to hand it off to someone instead of putting it in the garbage. It was *Dad's chair*. So I decide to sell it on Craigslist, that way I know where it's going. I look up the value of the two pieces online. The set is worth about a thousand dollars. On a Saturday morning, I list it for two-fifty. Priced to move. Looking for a good home. P.S., my father died in it.

A number of people reply to the ad, and I give them all my address because I feel insane. I buy a bottle of wine, and I buzz in anyone who shows up. There's a young couple, early twenties, fresh off the train from a private college in Maine, and they're furnishing their first apartment together, and they're so young and full of hope and I hate them and send them on their way. There's a woman named Adele who works in advertising, and she's snobby and looks me up and down and she actually gets on her hands and

knees and inspects the chair from underneath and complains about some scratches and then offers me a hundred
dollars less and I nearly scream at her as I escort her to the
door. Next, a leisurely retired couple, and this is their hobby,
just looking at people's furniture, wasting their time, taking their own stroll through the homes of New York City.
A dozen more people after that. They ask to use my bathroom; they dry their hands on my towel. They toss their
to-go cups in my garbage. They test out the chair, stretch
their legs on the ottoman. A recovering frat boy with no
taste of his own who has the impression this is the kind of
furniture he should want; he says, "It looks so retro." No,
pass, get out of my house. Underbidders, underachievers,
unlikable human beings. None of you are allowed to have
my father's chair.

Then there's Aaron, an aspiring folksinger, six months
in the city, who smells like weed. Curly-haired and open-
shirted. My father would have loved him for different reasons. Aaron would have listened raptly to the three Dylan
stories in my father's possession. My father loved to tell
those stories. Aaron tells me he's got a van downstairs, he
could take the chair right now, no problem. The van is for
touring, he says. He plays coffeehouses across America.
Folk music, he moved here for the folk scene, he says. Is
there a folk scene, I think but do not say out loud, oh wait I
did. "There is," he says and he laughs. "I like you," he says.
"You're a real ball buster." This seems to me to be his way

of reclaiming control of the conversation, acknowledging my critique but also de-feminizing me. He's dumb, and just another man. I don't care about his unbuttoned shirt anymore. He offers me two hundred dollars for the chair. "Bye-bye," I say.

"Come have coffee with me, then," he says. He glances at the bottle of wine, half empty. "Or a drink. Or whatever you want." He says I look like I need some fresh air. That's true. I walk outside with him. He points out the van. He says I should get in it. I do. We make out in the van for a while. "Let's get high," he says. "I don't want to," I say. "I'm already drunk. I don't need to." "I do," he says. He smokes weed from a one-hitter. "OK, all right," I say. I take a hit.

We go back upstairs to my apartment and fool around some more, and we get really close to having sex, I mean we are basically naked, I've got my underpants on, he's got his boxers on, but his dick is sticking out of them and is pressing up against me hard, and then he backs me onto the chair, and that's when I freak out. "I think you should leave," I tell Aaron. "This was too weird." "Are you sure?" he says. "We could just do it right now, super hard and fast, and then it will be over." He utters a string of filthy words, barely forming a sentence, but I get the idea. "No, go," I say. I don't feel threatened by him, but I get a little physical anyway, and I push him out the door. The action feels right. Then he disappears, presumably into the white-hot folk scene of New York City.

What was all that? My home was just ravaged by strangers. My body, too. I had made out with a man in a van. I had allowed all this to happen to me. I had invited this into my home. I could have just thrown that chair away and nothing bad would have happened. I feel deeply, physically ill. This fucking chair. I want it gone. Suddenly I remember the business card from the man who could do anything. I dig in my desk drawer, I dial the number. Alonzo picks up. I remind him who I am, that I'm my mother's daughter. "Evelyn's daughter, sure. Ev-e-lyn," he sings.

I tell him about the chair. "Do you think your friend would still want it?" I say. "Now let me think, who was that . . . Charlotte?" "I don't know if I ever knew her name," I say. "Yeah, it was Charlotte. I haven't seen her in a minute," he says. "I could track her down, but I don't think she'd want to hear from me. They come and they go, you know." "Yes," I say. This is the part I understand perfectly. (But am I a Charlotte? Or an Alonzo? Probably just an Andrea.) "Anyway I can take it off your hands," he says. "I can probably sell it if it's in good condition and all." "It's just been sitting here," I say. "Still intact." "I'll give you fifty bucks for it," he says. "Fine," I say. "Just take it." He tells me he's up in the Bronx, but he can get to Brooklyn after eight. I sit and drink the last of the wine until he knocks on my door.

"That's the chair all right," he says when he walks into the apartment. He runs his hand across the back of it. "Good as new," he says. "Some wear and tear," I admit. He pulls a billfold out of his pocket. The wad of cash is massive. "Honestly, I'd pay you fifty bucks to take it away," I say. "I don't ever want to see it again." I think: What's happening now? Oh, am I crying? I am. I wipe my eyes with the back of my hand. "You know what, honey, how about we do a trade instead?" he says.

He asks me to sit in the chair, and I do, gingerly, and then he rubs his hands together and closes his eyes, and then he tells me to close my eyes, and I do that, too. Then he takes his hands, which are warm, nearly hot, and places them on my leg for a while, and then on my arm, and then on my heart, and we talk while he does this, he asks me about my mother and my father and my brother, mostly about my mother, because he's fond of her, and then we talk about me, how old I am, what I do for a living, what makes me sad, what makes me happy, and I have a hard time answering these last two questions, I can't even remember the truth half the time, but as we discuss it, I start to feel a ball of heat gathering in my chest, above my breasts, just beneath my clavicle, and I hear Alonzo mutter, "There it is." Just when I think it can't get any hotter, the ball in my chest begins to recede, but only ever so slightly; still there is a distinct recession, and Alonzo pulls his hands away from my chest.

"I'm tired," I say. "I bet you are," he says. "You got a lot going on in there. I suggest you get it looked at a little more regularly. I'd do it but I don't come cheap," he says. "And

I can't be coming from the Bronx all the time. You should find someone local." We embrace, and then he takes the chair and the ottoman and leaves.

I watch him out the window on the street below. He lifts both pieces handily, as if they are feather light. He never needed Charlotte in the first place, I realize.

The next day I call a therapist. I see her a week later. I have been in therapy ever since. Eight years, I can't tell you if I've healed at all. If the pain Alonzo sensed that day under my skin has shrunk one bit. I like to think the swelling has gone down, and the heat has cooled. I like to think I'm better now. But most days I can't see through the pain to the truth.

Chloe

We meet at a mutual friend's barbecue, Baron and I. Our mutual friend's name is Deb, and she had told me in advance to look out for him. "Newly single," she had texted. "Like newly newly." "Fresh out of the womb," I texted back. "Successful, creative, smart," she texted. "A catch," I texted. "In a year he'll be a catch," she texted. "Right now he's a good time." "Am I not good enough for a catch?" I texted. She didn't text back for *six hours.* "Sorry," she texted. "Work." There was another pause. "Am I mistaken that you want to have a good time?" she texted. I had wanted to argue so badly but I couldn't.

Baron and I have an extremely long conversation about potato salad because Deb has made two kinds of potato salad, the creamy kind and the vinegary kind. It's a dumb, jokey conversation, kind of worthless actually, but he looks at me with obvious interest and desire. I get a little hot in my pants. He has a shaved head, the early male-pattern-baldness shave. He cleans his glasses a lot, and I point this out and he shrugs and says, "I can't stand fingerprints." I take his glasses from him, breathe on them, and wipe them on the end of my silky shirt. "Like new," I say, and hand them back. "You're helpful," he says. At some point in the conversation we realize we live ten blocks from each other. "Convenient," I say and grin.

Deb lives in a garden apartment, and there are children running in and out of the garden and the apartment, and one of them screeches and I shudder. "Children, ugh," I say. "I have a child," Baron says. "Just because I don't like children doesn't mean I can't like you," I say, and I touch his arm, and feel like both a failure and a success at the same time because even though I have already fucked this up, I was probably supposed to anyway.

Two normal people walk away from each other right then and there, but instead he gives me a ride home and parks in front of a fire hydrant on my street and then we make out in the front seat of his car, while I ignore the presence of the child seat in the back. He's really aggressive, tongue in the mouth, ear, throat, squeezing my breasts hard through my blouse. I'm both mortified and aroused. I put my hand on his dick through his pants and he stops and says, "You're the first person I've been with besides my ex-wife in twelve years." I say, "Whoa, that's a lot for a first date," and he says, "This wasn't a date," and I feel suddenly hoarse and damaged. "OK," I say. "I'm done." I put my hand on the door, but I give him a few seconds to apologize, which he does. He says, "I'm sorry, I don't know what I'm doing, I don't know if I'm coming or going. I'm having every emotion at once." He takes my hand and kisses it. "You're beautiful," he says. "You're beautiful and sexy and you should let me take you out and we'll do this right."

"Toxic," says my coworker Nina on Monday morning. "Drop him immediately."

He texts me on Wednesday and asks if I want to have dinner with him on Friday night. I say I have plans because I'm trying to play hard to get, which has absolutely never worked for me in my entire life. He says he can't see me on Saturday because he has his daughter that night. I fold instantly. "I'll move something around," I say. We pick a restaurant in the neighborhood, but it is a pretense because we both know what is going to happen. We've been texting about the things we're going to do to each other for days. It's terrible, and it's all I want.

On Friday I take off work early and get groomed in various ways, then I go to Dean & DeLuca and buy blueberries, and then I allow myself the indulgence of a MoMA visit. I pay twenty-five dollars and go up to the top floor and wend my way through the museum. Eventually I find myself lingering around their permanent collection. All that

work those people made for decades, and here's their greatest hits, one or two pieces plucked from storage. Better the
one piece than none at all, I guess. I miss painting. Even the
fumes I miss. I've spent the past thirteen years looking for a
smell to replace it.

Hours later I'm smelling all of him, his fumes. A cocktail at the bar before our reservation. I am thirty-eight and
he is forty-two. "I'm just starting over," he tells me. "Sometimes I feel like I'm done," I tell him. Dinner is fast, but I
still try to enjoy myself, because I love food; at the weirdest,
darkest, most stressful moments of my life, I always make
sure to have a nice meal. I order a steak. "I want it rare,"
I tell the waitress. "Like bloody red." "Carnivore," he says.
"That's me," I say. We drink two glasses of wine each, and I
say, "You know what we should have done?" and he says,
"Gotten the bottle?" "I never plan that right," I say, and he
says, "Me neither," and we smile at each other. Let's just get
along, I think. All we have to do is get along.

We walk to my apartment, not his, which he claims is a
mess. He is wearing a hat and a chambray shirt and shorts
and loafers and he has an easy stride. I am wearing a black
dress, loose and summery, and I feel pretty and intellectu-
ally engaged after my day of art. Also, I feel drunk. At home
there is bourbon, and I tell him that while we walk, and he
tells me I'm a dream girl. Like he literally says, "I feel like
you were sent to me as a present from the heavens above,"
and I laugh so hard but I *love* it.

When we get to my studio he surveys it and nods—the art, the stacks of books, the pots and pans dangling dramatically from a ceiling rack—while I shakily, excitedly pour us two bourbons, neat. We clink glasses and then drink quickly. "This is so exciting," he says. "I'm so excited." I boldly take off my dress. I'm just standing there naked in front of him. "I love all the curves," he says. "Hips. Yes." He is nodding at me, approving of me. I realize I am desperate for his approval. This man who was married, this father of one, someone else's, now mine.

He takes off his hat, and then his shirt, and then his pants. He is pale white and nearly hairless and I realize he has trimmed his pubic hair. "Did you—?" I point to his crotch. "I thought I was supposed to," he says. "I read it in *GQ*." "I really haven't seen it before," I say. "I think I went a little too far," he says. "I waxed my chest, too. It hurt." "I waxed too," I say. "Just here, though." I motion to my crotch. "It looks nice on you," he says. "Normal."

Our confessions done, we kiss, and then he's on me and it's fast, it's happening, it's on. He bends me over on my couch and, from behind, begins to pound me. There's a mirror nearby and I can see that he's watching himself, watching his facial expression. This moment has so little to do with me. After a while we try another position, and then another position, and then another position, and then another one. "Can we go back?" I say. "What? Huh?" he gasps, pushes his glasses up, looks at me. "I liked what we were doing before. Like ten minutes ago." "Hold on," he says, and he stops to clean his glasses with my nearby underpants.

Then we rearrange our bodies to the old position and we move very slowly and it's fantastic but then he starts to speed up and he goes faster and harder and it feels like he's trying to murder me with his dick and I say, "Slow down a little, baby," and he says, "I can't, I'm going to come, don't make me stop," so I don't because this is his first time fucking a person other than his wife in twelve years and it's with me, and I want him to remember it as great. I let him pound me for another minute and he orgasms, loud, certainly loud enough to be heard from the street below, and he's just so *proud* of himself, and almost immediately I begin to hate him, but also desire him even more, too.

I get myself off with a little assistance from him, an orgasm in a minor key, and then we sit at my kitchen table, naked, and eat blueberries, which have ripened since I bought them and left them in the sun by the window. I talk happily while I shove blueberries in my mouth. I'm always such an idiot after sex. At some point I realize he's stopped eating blueberries, and he's watching me eat, and I'm still eating, and then I finish the entire bowl. I sit back. "What?" I say. "I've got to go, I'm sorry," he says. He puts on all his clothes. I'm still naked. I'm just sitting there watching him make his exit. "Am I being weird?" he asks. "I don't know," I say. "*Are* you?" And then he's gone, no evidence left behind, except the light blue imprint of his fingers on my upper arm, which was where he held me too tightly.

The next day he apologizes via text for fucking me and leaving and I forgive him. We banter a bit about the sex we had. There is an acknowledgment that he is hard on one side of the conversation, and I am wet on the other side. Then he has to go: his kid is coming.

"How'd it go," asks Nina, Monday morning, first thing.

"He freaked out and left after sex," I say.

"Oh well," says Nina.

"How'd it go," texts Deb.

"He's really nice!" I text back.

"Do you like him?" she says.

I don't reply.

Baron and I volley texts back and forth for a few days about seeing each other again. No specific plans are made. Just: Let's hang out soon.

The next week I see him on the street. He's walking with his daughter, holding her hand with one hand, and a plastic bag of groceries with the other, the green stems of carrots poking out the top of the bag. She is wearing a blue-flow-ered backpack. Her mother must be of Hispanic descent. She is a beautiful little girl. Baron sees me coming from a block away, waves, and then crosses to the other side of the street.

"How dare you," I text him later.

"You told me you hate children," he texts back.

We still have sex sometimes, can you believe it? I have grown to hate him more and more as time passes, and he, me. We are cruel to each other in bed sometimes. Nasty and forceful. I want him regardless, or because of it. Was there a moment we could have brought out the best in each other? Was that ever a possibility? Could we have taken another path? When I think about all the little intersections in our time together I wonder when we could have gone left or right instead of straight ahead, into the pile of mud we're stuck in together.

Once I run into him when he's with another woman. It's a Sunday, and I'm having breakfast by myself in a café after reading the paper in the park. Last bit of coffee in the cup, sweet and milky. It's a sunny day. In an hour I'll call my mother, in another hour I'll call my brother and his wife and ask about their sick child. Sundays are the days I am the most me I will ever be.

Then he walks in with her, and they are in old T-shirts and jeans and her hair is a mess and they are casual and comfortable with each other. There is nowhere else in the café to sit. I see him see me, and I see him suggest they find another place, and I see her say, "But there's a table right there." She plops down next to me, a freshly fucked inno-cent. I just wanted an omelet, not an assassination attempt. I signal for the bill. I wave that waiter down like I'm in the middle of nowhere on the side of a road with a flat tire. Help, I wave. Help me.

"Hi," Baron says.

"Nope," I say. The woman watches us both. Never mind the check. I throw down a twenty and leave. Let him explain me to her.

Once he says, "I can't see you anymore. I'm ruining my life, the shit that I'm doing."

Once he tries to talk about his daughter to me. Her name is Chloe. I tell him to shut up. "You don't get to talk to me about her," I say. And he never mentions her again.

SIGRID

When I was twenty-five years old I flew from Chicago to New York City to visit my brother, David. He was twenty-nine and he was in another band that was doing all right, better than fine, not great, not yet. He couldn't quit his crappy day job or anything. But I thought he was the coolest person in the world. He'd been in three great bands before that, a musical influencer if not influential. And even though we lived far away from each other, I wanted desperately to be a part of his life.

Everyone in the band was young and good-looking, so they had been in a bunch of magazines, not just reviews but a few fashion shoots, too, modeling spring looks, and then a few months later, modeling fall looks. On one of those shoots my brother met a magazine editor named Greta, who was a few years older than him. She had lustrous blond hair and clothes that designers gave her for free because she looked so willowy and thin and graceful in them, but also she wore these intense, blue-rimmed glasses because she wanted to make sure you knew she was smart.

They began to date and they fell in love and soon after that they moved in together. (My mother, at the time: "What's the rush?") This is when I showed up for a visit, two months after they had moved to the Lower East Side. Their street was shit: there was a grimy bodega with crumbling linoleum floors, a group of angry, husky-voiced men hanging around outside it; my brother presumed drugs were sold there, though he never actually bought any, preferring to work only with the same delivery service he'd been using since high school. But the apartment was new inside, all hardwood everything, and the walls were decorated with art from their friends, up-and-coming artists, and a few older pieces Greta had inherited. Everything was framed and very professional-looking except for the tag on the wall outside their bathroom, which Greta assured me had been done by a very famous graffiti artist during their housewarming party, an act that she viewed as good luck for their new home.

That weekend they had another party, a smaller one, for my benefit. I got drunk and also did some coke and slept with one of my brother's bandmates. We snuck out together but not gracefully and everyone saw us making out on the fire escape first anyway. I realize now this was a pathetic attempt to grab on to a bit of their glamour, this ill-advised fucking. But also he was very handsome, half real Italian, with dark hair in loose waves and chest hair by the fistful. On the surface, who could blame me?

And yet it created a small rift between my brother and this bandmate and ultimately the other bandmates. For a period of time my brother did not speak to me, until Greta stepped into the fray and brokered a peace treaty, resulting from a long phone call during which he asked me point-blank if I thought I was an alcoholic and I said, "No, I'm just *young* and *having fun*." Followed by tears, choking-sob tears, and I made sure he heard it. And he said, "Can you just put a pin in it when you're in my world?" I agreed to put a pin in it. The band broke up anyway, and my brother ended up forming another band, which, with Greta's help and connections, ended up being even more successful than the previous one. Half of the songs he wrote were about Greta, and my brother called this band "my new baby," named it, coddled it, and we were all charmed by his sweetness toward his music and also toward Greta. (By then my mother had decided she liked Greta, perhaps more than she liked me, although she *loved* me more.) And so his sister's decadent ways were forgiven, all was forgiven, especially because something good came out of it in the end.

After a series of terrible relationship dramas in Chicago, one in particular involving an academic superior, I dropped out of graduate school, hung out in the city shamefacedly for a while, skimming the bottom of the Wicker Park alcoholic fish tank, until Greta finally invited me to move into their apartment for the summer. David would be on tour and she wanted the company. And my family was worried about me, which was not explicitly stated but certainly understood, especially when I arrived, bloated and hung over, at their apartment to find my mother waiting for me with Greta, the two of them eating ridiculous, dainty cucumber and cheese sandwiches as if that were something they would ever eat. *Join us in civilization,* they seemed to be saying with those sandwiches. I ate six of them, and blamed it on all the travel, but really it was because I hadn't eaten anything vaguely normal in weeks.

What followed that summer was a sequence of events worthy of a humanitarian award: Greta nursed me back to health, contending with my (1) minor drug addiction, (2) active nervous breakdown, and (3) discovery of a (treatable) venereal disease, while at the same time securing freelance work for me, a person who'd had, up until that time, only restaurant work on her résumé. Girlfriend of the Year Award goes to Greta Johannson, for bringing the art school dropout cokehead back to life, while the long-term serious boyfriend (but not yet fiancé!) traveled around Europe in a van, spending his nights smoking hash with all of his new best friends he met at rock shows. Saint Greta of the Lower East Side.

Eventually I moved to Brooklyn, after I got the job I have now. David and his band stayed on tour for another year. They barely broke even. When he was in New York, he temped to help supplement the rent, but we all knew Greta was supporting him. I don't think being out of money bothered him much; we'd always struggled as a family, squeezing every last penny out of our food stamps. And he got to go all over the world. The stories he told! Greta flew to meet him in Japan, a place she had never been and had always been dying to visit. He went on to Australia and New Zealand, and when he came home he proposed to Greta. She said yes, of course.

They had their wedding on a farm upstate. The only parent present was my mother; our father, the gray-haired intellectual/jazz musician/junkie, deceased now for years, as were Greta's parents, heart attack, cancer, too young their deaths, which was not a thing they said about my father, who had been asking for it for a long time. At the reception Greta toasted them in absentia and everyone cried, even the people who had never known them. The bride wore flowers in her hair, the groom went tieless, and I slept with another of David's bandmates, although this time nobody found out.

A few months after they got married, at a crowded Thanksgiving dinner, Greta announced she was pregnant.

(My mother shrieked.) Here was the plan: David would not go back to his low-paying temp work. Instead he was going to do a solo album and promote it himself so he could work out of the house most days. He had friends who made a better living taking control of their own careers, rather than leaving it in the hands of record companies, who had no idea what to do with someone like him anyway. He would take care of the baby solo, too. Greta would continue to work at the magazine, where she had now risen, in part due to her stoic Nordic nature in the face of drama.

Greta took all her prenatal vitamins and glowed through her pregnancy. Her hair grew as thick as a lion's mane. At her baby shower I held her hair in my hand. "It's not human," I said. "It's something else," my brother said. It was a month before the baby was due. "Are you so ready?" I asked. I sipped my third mimosa of the afternoon. "I am," she said. She rubbed her enormous belly. "Come out soon, little baby. We are ready to meet you."

A month later Greta delivered a baby girl. They named her Sigrid after Greta's mother. Sigrid was very sick from the beginning. She had a congenital heart defect, small, rare, and undetectable. Almost immediately she suffered a series of strokes, one of which damaged her brain. She was not quite lifeless. Technically, she was alive. Her doctor said she had about three years to live, perhaps five if she was lucky. ("What does any of this have to do with luck?" said my mother.) The baby was set up to fail before she had even begun.

For the first few years of her life, I tried to know this child. I held her hand as she lay, unmoving, flat on her back on a small pad on the table in my brother's kitchen, on Sunday nights, so that Greta and David could have a moment alone together in public, a glass of wine at a bar, a stiff drink to keep them erect. I talked to Sigrid and told her about my day. But I didn't feel like she heard me, or recognized me. She was both unknowable and incapable of knowing. Greta and David believed they understood her, though. I thought they were fooling themselves.

My brother did the best he could. The baby needed all manner of assistance: food through a tube, shots, salves, hugs, prayers. They were cautious about taking her out in a stroller, she was so delicate, so tiny; David was often housebound with her. "I thought I was going to be one of those dads in the park with their kid," he said to me once, in a rare admission of sadness. "Cool dad in the park," I said. "With the cool sunglasses." "I was going to be the coolest dad of all," he said.

Greta's magazine folded. On top of that, no one was buying David's new record because people had stopped buying any records at all. Touring was impossible. Who would take care of Sigrid? Greta found freelance work, but she was just a hired hand and had no flexibility in her schedule anymore. My mother was still working: she had two more years to go, although she offered to retire early to help, but Greta said no, absolutely not, because that's Greta. They couldn't afford much childcare; their savings were easily depleted. We were a family falling apart, the Berns were. We still loved each other, but individually we were all in trouble. No one was happy, no one was healthy. And I can't speak for anyone else, but I was drinking like a fish.

Then, out of nowhere, a distant relative of Greta's died, leaving her a small sum of money and a house in New Hampshire. There was a respected pediatric hospital about an hour away, near Dartmouth. After little discussion, they decided to move. (My mother was not happy. NOT HAPPY.) They were exhausted with the city, with their lives there, and whatever they had gotten out of it by being a young creative beautiful couple was no longer available to them. They gave up their apartment, packed up their art and books and musical instruments and their eternally sleeping baby, and moved to a small town where they knew no one but each other. If you asked Greta it was a fresh start, and if you asked David it was purgatory, but either way, they both agreed: New York City was hell.

I helped them move up there. David handled the U-Haul, and I drove the station wagon they had purchased hurriedly off Craigslist. Greta, watching over the baby, sat in the back seat. We pulled up early in the morning. It was January, and there was a mountain of snow on the ground, big puffy white piles of it, but someone had cleared a path down the small gravel road that led to the house. I inched forward slowly, so as to keep the ride smooth for the baby, but still there were little pops and grooves in the road. With each jerk Greta winced in the back seat.

The house was a crumbling brick monster, uneven in appearance. It had one story with a bright red door at its center. I got out of the car and David got out of the van. I trudged through the snow on one side of the house and he on the other. There was a mountain in the distance, and a small set of woods nearby. The trees were barren, yet they were so dense I couldn't see much past the first row. There was a gray sky above, a rich moist color, not gloomy at all, nearly purple.

David was staring at a small, rotting shack next to the house. "Where the fuck am I?" he said. "Do I live here now? I have a shack. Look at my shack." It wasn't purgatory anymore: he had his own playroom. I watched as he carried his record player and crates of vinyl straight into the shack.

Later Greta drove me to the train station in Portsmouth. I had made plans for that night to see an old boyfriend, Alex, from my undergraduate days in Boston. We'd been texting steadily for a month, ever since I had found out I was going to New Hampshire. He'd had one marriage, and it had been short, brutal, and intense, like a punk song that kept ringing in his ears. He'd been telling me that he wanted to buy me a steak dinner. The juicy steak soon became a metaphor for something else in our communications. It was disgusting. I didn't care. My brother had a sick baby and my mother was depressed and I hated my job in addition to other significant features of my life. I would be his steak, if that was what it took.

Greta thanked me and held me tightly and I could smell the sweat from the day on her. She was wearing new glasses, bifocals, no makeup, a sweatshirt, jeans; the old Greta was gone. "You know what the hardest part about all of this is?" she said. "Leaving our family behind." "We're always going to be here for you," I said. "Just a phone call away. Or a really long drive. But probably not on a holiday weekend, because traffic's going to be a bitch." "Please don't kid around like that," she said. "Promise you'll come visit." She grabbed my hands. "Promise you'll come and see her," she said. I promised. Then I got on the train to Boston.

That was two years ago. I haven't seen Alex since, though sometimes we text, and once he asked me to send him a naked picture, and I laughed and laughed, so for that I thank him, because who doesn't need a good laugh? And I've only seen David and Greta and Sigrid a few times since they've left town, but mostly I have found myself resisting their sadness when I have so much of my own. Everything was quiet, though not silent, between us. I wanted to believe everything was fine. I asked them to come visit, so did my mother, but there was always a reason why they couldn't, and then they stopped offering reasons entirely, so we stopped asking for them. I talk to my brother once a week, his voice a low, calm rumble. The house behind him is quiet, there's no street noise, no sirens, no cars, no tough

New Yorkers arguing a floor below. I imagine the air in their house just hovering, sweet, static, calm air. Greta posts pictures of their garden on Facebook, the seeds she is planting, all labeled in a row. He took a picture of her, squinting in a sun hat, crouching by the dirt. "New babies," she wrote next to it. There were no pictures of Sigrid posted. Just other forms of life, growing in the earth.

INDIGO HAS A BABY

Indigo has a baby and I don't go to see it for a long time. It's not that I don't care about seeing her baby, it's that I don't care about seeing any baby. Also I know what will happen. I have been down this road before. Once I see the baby I will have *seen* the baby. I need to see the baby when it is little, so that someday when I see the baby when it is grown or at least not a baby anymore I can say, "I remember you when you were *this* big." It's all a setup for a later scene to occur at a holiday party, or in a café, or, realistically, on a street corner, two grown women nodding enthusiastically at the size of an uninterested child tugging on its mother's hand. Once you were small. Now you are big.

"Why haven't you come to see the baby yet?" says Indigo. A message she leaves on the phone. Noncombative, but making a point. Wheedling. Not a question she actually

wants answered. "I'll be home all day. I don't ever go anywhere. It's just me and the baby. So just come over. We'll be
here."

What will happen after I see the baby is that Indigo will
become exceedingly busy with her life for a very long time.
Say, five years or so. Then she will have time again to see
me. Then she will desperately need to see me. Where has
the time gone? What have I been doing? Oh, yes, parenting.
But by then I will be a different version of me (or, worse,
perhaps the same version) and she will be a different version of her and we will look at each other with different
eyes. You had a baby and I didn't and here we are. Do you
remember when . . . ? Yes! Yes. Sure.

I text her back so I don't have to answer her specific
question, the rhetorical status of it unclear. I say, "I'll come
on Saturday." I break brunch plans with my mother, and I
move my morning session with my therapist an hour earlier.

I know the minute I go to see that baby, my friendship
with Indigo is over. I liked being friends with her. She was
my most beautiful friend, physically, spiritually. She was always so healthy. She quit corporate America to become a
yoga instructor and she stopped eating anything that came
from a cow, and it showed in her tingling white teeth and
her lustrous, enormous hair and her skin, which glowed a
luxurious caramel color. Any ailment I had, she could suggest an herbal remedy for it. Or a specific stretch. Indigo
and me, doing backbends in her living room, my blood rac-

ing to my face, and I'm thinking: I always wanted a friend like this. I will miss those backbends, Indigo. They really did help with my stress.

I go to a children's store in my neighborhood, pink, chirpy, cheerful, and buy the baby a book, *The Giving Tree*, a dire story about a selfish child sucking the life out of an enabling tree. (That tree has no agency, is what I've always thought.) But that is the book you buy a baby. I'm certain Indigo has five copies of it already. I'm too late to be the first at anything. I also buy a stuffed rabbit, its floppy ears draping softly in a sea of pastel tissue paper inside the gift bag. This, too, I know she has multiple versions of, more or less. There is nothing original I can offer this child. I am obligated to make an offering, however, a virgin to the gods, a stuffed animal to a new baby. If I lay this gift on the altar, will you promise me I'll never get pregnant? I make sure to get gift receipts for both.

At the therapist's office, I am hostile, and physically awkward, head hanging low, shoulders slumped, hunched over at the waist in the dark leather chair. I could have sat on the couch, but I would like to resist all temptation to curl into the fetal position and die. And that's what the couch is saying to me. Sit on me and die.

This is only the fourth time I've visited my therapist in the past six months. She has been leaving me voice mail messages, suggesting I set up an appointment. "Why don't you check in?" she says. Now I'm here and I can't look her in the eye. *Isn't it enough that I'm in your office?* is what I want to say to her. *Don't I get points for making it in the first place? And now you want me to perform, too?*

I'll admit that each time I've seen her I've spilled my guts and felt cleansed. Then I become convinced I never need to see her again. Soon enough my well fills and she seems to know just as it's reached its brim, and that's when she phones me. I don't pick up, ever. I let her talk into the air. Let her stew. I don't know why I'm mad at her. She's just doing her job. But shouldn't I feel better by now? It's been seven years.

She asks me how I've been. Job, adequate; brother, terrible; I feel closer to my mother lately, and that's been nice, but the whole family is devastated about my brother's sick baby. We talk about my love life. She always tries to figure out what I want from a man, from a relationship. She asks me point-blank: "What do you want? Until you know what you want you're not going to find it." She's giving me tough love. I think: You don't know anything about tough, lady. Then I tell myself: You don't know anything about love.

I don't answer her directly. Instead I go through all the men in my life for her. There is a man I knew years ago, an artist, struggling, whimsical, pleasant, broke. I do not take him seriously as a potential love interest, but sometimes we meet for drinks. There is a former neighbor I text with and sometimes he comes over and we drink wine on my roof. He won't date me because I'm white and he's black and he refuses to date white girls but I think maybe we're dating anyway. There is a newly single man, a divorced dad ten blocks away. I met him at a barbecue and we've had sex a few times, and he pounds into me like he's going for a gold medal in fucking. Whenever I leave him I am shaken, off-kilter, yet I always return when he calls.

"If you add them all up they equal a boyfriend," I say. "No, they don't," she says. "Half a boyfriend, then," I say. She says nothing. There is a notebook on her lap. She writes nothing in it. Finally I start to cry. "I don't understand why you won't just leave me alone," I say. I wish I were on that couch, I think. That couch looks great.

The therapist asks me if I want to make another appointment with her and I tell her I'll call her when I know my schedule better and I am lying to her and we both know it. Before I leave her office I go to the bathroom so that I can drop Visine in my eyes. I would die if Indigo knew I was sad when I went to visit the baby. We should all be happy about the baby when we see it. The baby is unspoiled and perfect and doesn't need to know anything about a lack of direction in life or family crises or inappropriate sexual partner choices.

Indigo lives in Tribeca, in a loft on the top floor of a small, old, beautiful building, full of tiny, romantic architectural details and two enormous pillars in the living room. She is draped on her couch when I enter, swathed in white, flowing fabrics. It's unclear if what she's wearing is a dress or separate shirt and pants or what. Where does one garment end and the other begin? An old-fashioned metal fan, erect on a stand, blows nearby. The fabric surrounding her flutters in its breeze. Swaddled in the middle of this is a baby boy. He is not as dark-skinned as his mother, but still tan, and his hair is a striking platinum blond.

"Look at him, he's perfect," I say, and he is. "A little drop of heaven."

Indigo gives a dazed smile. "Forgive me, I just finished my morning meditation," she says. "Also my mother just went back to Trinidad and I'm trying to recall who I once was before she took over my apartment. She hates New York, really hates it, so she refuses to leave the house once she gets here. She just wants to be with the baby. I beg her to take a walk but she says, 'Where would I go?' I don't know, Mom, what would you possibly want to see in New York City? In this whole wide beautiful world, what would you want to see?"

Oh, Indigo, I shall miss you, I think. When you crack, you crack beautifully.

And then she remembers something, remembers how she wants to be in the universe. Yogi Indigo. "I'm always happy for the help, of course. She gifts me with her time and I am grateful. I am . . ." She looks at her child, deeply, nearly lustily. Don't say it, I think. "Blessed," she sighs.

But, I think, I shall survive without you.

Her baby's name is Efraim. "That's an old man's name," I say. "Like a dead old man from the Bible."

"We were going to call him Tyler but then we looked into his eyes when he was born and he seemed one thousand years old already and I said *Efraim*. The wisdom of all the ages in one head."

"Do you like it?" I ask. "Having a baby, being a parent?"

"I feel like my whole universe has folded itself in and then out again, renewing my soul and my mind."

I laugh at Indigo, and she blinks and smiles. She doesn't think any of this is funny. She is on Planet Indigo, and I am merely making a visit there.

"What does Todd think?" I ask.

Todd is an investment banker. Todd's all right. He's *fine*. He's originally from Seattle and he was nearly a doctor instead of a banker and he started a microfinancing business to help children in Tunisia, a country he visited as a volunteer in college, back when he was a Christian. When he stopped being a Christian he lit his soul on fire in Tribeca for a decade using his Wall Street money as the kindling. Then he met Indigo, and now they are doing this thing, with the loft, and the marriage, and the baby.

"Todd's in love with our Efraim. *In love*. Really, you've never seen a man more smitten with his own child. Before work every morning he gets up and takes him for a walk around the neighborhood. He shows him off everywhere he goes. It's darling."

The baby cries. Indigo reaches into the many folds of her fabric and somehow quite easily pulls out an enormous breast, with a giant, erect nipple. Her garments waft around her. She attaches her child to her nipple.

"What about you?" she says. "What about your life? Tell me what the rest of the world is doing. I'm dying to know."

"I just went to my therapist," I say.

"I didn't know you were back in therapy," she says.

"I'm not," I say. "Well, I'm dabbling. I don't know. I guess what's old is new."

The baby smacks loudly at her tit.

"It's just good to have someone to talk to sometimes."

"You don't need to sell me on therapy. Todd and I have been going since our six-month anniversary. That was his present to me. He got us an appointment with the best couples counselor in town."

The baby sucks and sucks.

"We talk about my relationships mostly," I say. "This woman and I."

"That's good," she says.

"I don't really have a relationship, though," I say. "I have just bits and pieces of things."

"That's a start," she says. She strokes the baby's head.

"I think I'm just going to be alone forever," I say. I am starting to get upset.

"It's fine if you want to be alone," she says.

"I don't know if I want to be alone, I just think I'm going to be," I say. Well, most of the time I do. It's complicated. I don't see myself as having anything conventional. But still I date. I fuck. I seek.

"You don't have to be with anyone. It doesn't define your worth," she says, in her two-million-dollar loft that her husband bought.

"I know that," I say.

People architect new lives all the time. I know this because I never see them again once they find these new lives. They have children or they move to new cities or even just to new neighborhoods or you hate their spouse or their spouse hates you or they start working the night shift or they start training for a marathon or they stop going to bars or they start going to therapy or they realize they don't like you anymore or they die. It happens constantly. It's just me. I haven't built anything new. I'm the one getting left behind.

"You're never really alone anyway. You have people all around you," she whispers. "And energy, too." Indigo has always been one of my biggest fans.

She unlatches the baby and puts him to her shoulder. While she burps him, she studies me. It's then I realize I have been crying the entire time. Unfair! I wouldn't have cried if I hadn't gone to therapy first. That loosened the gears. It's not my fault, I want to tell Indigo. It's someone else's fault.

Indigo offers me a glass of wine, but I say no because

it's eleven a.m., even though yes, obviously, I would love a glass of wine, nearly all the time.

"I'm fine. I've just been going from zero to sixty lately for no reason at all."

"It took you so long to come and see me, I thought something must be wrong. Or that maybe you were mad at me."

"Nothing's wrong," I say. "I could not tell you one thing that is wrong with my life except that it is exactly the same."

She offers me the baby. "Here," she says. "Hold Effy. He's the best picker-upper I know." I would rather have a glass of wine. But I hold Effy. And he is all the things you want a baby to be. He smells like sweet cream and his hair is petal-soft. All right, show me what you got, kid, I think; let's see what you know. Indigo coos in the background, the fan shuddering behind her. I look into his eyes. She promised me wisdom. I do not see the wisdom of the ages. But, for a moment, in the tenderness of this baby's existence, in his blank and gentle ease, I see the relief.

You don't know anything yet, I think. You don't know a goddamn thing. You lucky baby.

Evelyn

My mother tells me she's moving. She finally retired, and she's going to New Hampshire to help my brother, David, and his wife, Greta, take care of their sick child, Sigrid, who is four years old and dying, who might die soon. They live in a small town where there are no Jews, a thing that might be important to my mother, so I point it out. She shrugs. "Grandchild trumps Jews," she says. We are eating whitefish salad and bagels downtown, a thing we do most Saturdays now, meet in the middle between my house and her house. What about whitefish, I want to say. Do they have whitefish in New Hampshire? And what about me? What do I trump?

She starts talking about her plans for her apartment, which is rent-stabilized. Without it, we never would have survived our poverty-stricken childhood. She can't give it up, I tell her. It has to live on in our family forever. I always thought I'd get it someday, or that David would come back. "I'll leave it empty," she says. "For now." While she's talking about what she'll take with her and what she'll leave behind, I experience a minor panic attack. "But I don't know when I'll be back," she says. "It could be a year. It could be three. Maybe never." I stop eating. I push my plate forward. "Maybe I'll love New Hampshire, stranger things have happened, all those trees and fresh air." I'll never see her again. Now I'll have to make fun of the people who scoop out their bagels all by myself. Criminals, my mother calls them.

"Andrea, don't waste that, that's good whitefish," my mother says. "You eat it," I say. "You're going to miss it when it's gone." "They have food in New Hampshire," she says.

I am struck by this feeling that she will die in New Hampshire. New York City is her electrical socket. Her friends, the streets, the trains, the restaurants, the parks, the museums, the myriad free lecture series available. My mother loves lectures. She and her best friend Betsy from her activist days go to at least three a week, the two of them with their shining gray hair, sitting front and center, Betsy, childless Betsy, knitting another scarf for charity, my mother nodding and taking notes, which she sometimes types up and emails to me and some of her friends the next day. "Just thought I'd share what I learned last night," every email starts. Forget the whitefish, forget me, what about the lectures?

"Don't leave me," I say. "Change is good," she says. "Change is terrible," I say. "You've had me long enough," she says. I eat the whitefish.

A conversation with my therapist:

ME: My mother is leaving me and moving to New Hampshire.

THERAPIST: And how does that make you feel?

ME: It makes me feel like she doesn't love me.

THERAPIST: Hasn't she proved to you she loves you already?

ME: How?

THERAPIST: By caring for you, nurturing you, supporting you, raising you to be the person you are today.

ME: All of that comprises a rational argument but can I just ask you a question?

THERAPIST: Sure.

ME: Whose side are you on, anyway?

A few weeks later I offer to rent a car and drive her to New Hampshire, even though I object, I object, I object!

She has two suitcases and a few boxes of personal possessions, which I poke through when I arrive at her apartment. It's mostly books on parenting and grandparenting and a few books on faith. There are also copies of *The Feminine Mystique* and *The Prophet*, which seem dated when I consider how studious and forward thinking my mother has been for her entire life. I stand there, holding them. "It comforts me that they're near," she says. I wave them at her. "Old Betty and Kahlil, who knew?" I say. "They remind me of a certain time," she says. "They remind me of your father." "OK," I say. "Let's just go," she says. She hustles us both out of the apartment, leaves it locked, airless, dark, for the time being.

We listen to NPR for the first two hours on the road, the strange comfort of bad news reported in reasonable tones, my mother sliding in and out of commentary. She buys pretty much everything NPR is selling, but she has her moments of doubt: some reports seem superficial to her. "What would they do if they had more time with that story?" she wonders. "Two more minutes on the lives of the people who grow the vegetables we eat, would it kill them?" I ignore her.

She makes me pull in for coffee at a rest stop in Connecticut. "Let's sit for a second, come here, sit with me, my dear daughter," she says. I slump in a booth. "You haven't said two words this whole trip." "I don't feel like talking," I say. "I'm sad you're leaving, that's all."

"You know, you didn't even like me very much until your thirties," she says.

"Well, that's true," I say. "It was hard sometimes, growing up in our house."

"I had a rough ride with your father," she says. "It took me a long time to recover."

"I'm not asking for an explanation," I say. I think about all the dinner parties she had after Dad died. All the men in the house. All those laps I sat on. All the attention.

"I'm just saying you've lived without me appearing regularly in your life before, you'll do it again," she says.

"Who are you trying to console at this exact moment?" I say.

Before we get back on the road, we use the restroom, which reeks of disinfectant, and I gag. A teenage girl grudgingly mops the handicapped stall. My mother stays behind for five extra minutes to discuss the local union situation with the girl. I go to the car and text every single person I know the following sentence: "My mother is trying to murder me with her emotions. Please send help."

When we cross the Massachusetts state line she says, "There's something we need to discuss."

"No," I say. "I'm not having a discussion with you now. I'm all out of discussion energy."

"Andrea."

"Fine."

"If I ever get sick, like really sick, and I need someone to pull the plug on me, I want you to be the one."

"What? No. I don't want to talk about this."

"I'm asking you to do this for me," she says. "This is part of being an adult, facing issues of mortality."

"Then why doesn't David have to do it?" I say.

"David has his own issues of mortality," says my mother. "His own trials and tribulations. It's time for you to have yours."

"I have many problems, I promise you," I say.

"Also I don't trust him to respect my wishes. But I know you could do it when the time comes."

"What makes you think I could do it?"

"Haven't you wanted to kill me your entire life?" she says.

"Ha-ha," I say.

"Ha-ha," she says.

"Why are we having so many sad conversations lately?" I say.

"This is what happens when you get older. You have to think about sickness and death and dying and all of that. I had to do it with Nana and Papa. I was the plug-puller too, if it makes you feel any better. It doesn't make you a bad person or a good person. It just means you're *capable*."

We drive for two more hours, get off the fast highway onto a slower one, then a slower, winding road. We drive past lakes littered with fallen leaves, crushed, choking the violet-tipped water. This could be a pleasure trip. Nearly a getaway. The roads grow smaller, four lanes, then two, sometimes just one; shorter buildings, then fewer buildings;

long stretches of only grass and trees; the skies echo blue
for miles. Tractors, goats, fir trees, chicken coops, a lawn
mower. A small cemetery.

I tell my mother we'll be there in ten minutes.

"Oh, we forgot to talk about your love life," says my
mother.

"Save it, lady," I say.

We're in the woods now, and I can hear every pop of
gravel under the tires as I pull up to their house. My sister-
in-law, blond, healthy, bigger than usual, hairier too, opens
the front door with a finger to her lips. The baby is sleeping. The baby is always sleeping, I want to tell Greta. The
baby has a terrible heart and a damaged brain and she has
never uttered a word. I don't believe she has ever been truly
awake in her life. Instead I whisper back a hello, and I kiss
her, and my mother throws her arms around her and we all
walk through the crumbling brick house in the woods together to see the baby. I diverge, and ask where my brother
is, and Greta points to the backyard. She mimes playing a
guitar, rolls her eyes a little bit while doing so. I wander in
the direction of wherever the baby isn't.

Behind the house, from the small shack, I can hear a
guitar being strummed. I knock on the door. Butterflies in a
haze around the edges of the shack, green, green grass, blue
skies, looming, enormous trees at the edge of the property,
a creek beyond it, my brother showed it to me once. "It's
me," I say. "Your sister." He's playing a guitar solo, I think.

I should wait until he's done. Then I realize everything's a guitar solo when you're playing by yourself, and I enter.

Inside is recording equipment, a laptop, a patterned sheet tacked to the wall, and a mattress on the floor, on which my brother sprawls, his ears covered in headphones, a guitar in his arms. His beard is enormous and fully gray. He has shaved his balding head clean. The shack smells faintly of weed. I wave a hand in front of his face. "You're here," he says. He seems both delighted and desperate. He takes off his headphones, stands, and then mauls me with a hug.

My brother calls himself a lifer when he talks about his music. He was never going to become famous—that we knew. Famous is hard, and anyway, you're not supposed to want it; raw, apparent desire for it is disgusting, my brother has told me. "Making good music is the thing you're supposed to want," he says. "Watching people dance to it or sing along or just love it, their faces at the shows. That's part of fame, sure, but not all of fame, and you can have that anyway, without being famous." He makes music and sells it over the internet and a few times a year he plays free shows in New York and his gray-haired, balding fans come out and join him and buy his merch and get drunk with him and post his picture with them on the internet, as if someone had seen a ghost and captured a fleeting image and wanted to prove it was true. "I can't do this forever," says my brother. "I mean the music will live on, but eventually I'll have no one left to come to my shows. They'll all die." "So will you," I say. "And so will you," he says.

We vape. He plays me some of his music. I ask him how his little girl is doing and he tells me it's the same, the same, always the same. "How are you and Greta doing?" I say. He scratches his beard, rubs his eyes, pats his bald scalp, like fully interacts with his head in all ways possible, then says, "Sometimes she thinks Sigrid is getting better. So that's weird." "Sigrid is never getting better," I say. "I know," he says. "Sigrid is only ever getting worse," I say. "You don't need to tell me that," he says.

Eventually we leave the shack and wend our way back to the house. The butterflies have disappeared, and now it's just gnats and a preamble to the sunset. A bunny hops in the distance. "It's pretty here," I tell my brother. "It must be a nice life." He puts his arm around me. "I'm miserable," he says. My mother and Greta stand at the screen door. My mother is holding the baby, slack in her arms. A four-year-old who never grew much. Greta's eyes are sad and enormous. "But Mom's here now," he says. "And I think that's going to help."

After dinner, when the stars have come out and I have drunk all the wine available in the house, my mother and I share the guest room. Which, technically, is her room now, I guess. Before we go to bed I tell her I know what she's doing, that she gave her time to me and now she's giving her time to David. "But what I really want to know is, what about you?" I say.

"I've had enough me to last a lifetime," my mother says. She's facing the wall and her voice is dreamy. Then she tells me she loves me, she tells me to go to sleep. "In the morning we'll have a new day," she says. "That's the best part of going to sleep. Knowing there's a new day tomorrow."

"That's the kind of thing you tell a child," I say. "I expect more from you."

"Andrea, enough!" she snaps. "You know, you're doing better than you think you are. You can survive without me."

"I'm not," I say.

"All right, even if you're not, which I don't believe is true, just grow up already," she says. She flips over, and her voice is closer to me. "Handle your shit, Andrea. You're thirty-nine years old. You can do it."

"I'll try," I say.

"One more thing," my mother says. "I see you not holding that baby. You think I don't notice it, but I do."

I say absolutely nothing.

"Tomorrow you hold the baby," she says.

I'm the sick baby, I think. Me. Who will hold me?

In the morning I leave early, before anyone else in the house is awake. I write a note that says, "Work emergency," and then I throw it away because no one will believe me; everyone knows I hate my job and I find nothing urgent about it. I write another note that says, "Dear family, See you soon, thank you, I love you," noncommittal, truthful, sweet, then I draw a heart at the bottom. I walk out back to see the birds and the trees and the sky in the early-morning sun, and all of it is orchestral, I'm relieved that it exists, this beauty. Light music plays in the shack. I knock on the door. My brother opens it, in his pajamas. "Oh David," I say. I hug him goodbye, and he sobs into my neck. "All right, all right," I say. "You can have her."

THE LAST MAN ON EARTH

I go to an art show. It's a solo exhibit for my friend
Matthew. He was briefly my boyfriend when we were both
in graduate school, when I was still an artist, or aspired to
be one, "artist" as a job title, anyway, but that was thirteen
years ago, and whatever we both were back then we are
not now.

Matthew is absurdly tall, six feet five, something like
that, and thin, and breakable, and a sad sack. His art reflects
both his treetop view of the world and his mournful tem-
perament: he makes a lot of paintings about looking down
into centers, holes, dark depths. "Are you OK?" is what I always want to say to him when I see his work, but that's a
rude question to ask another artist unless you're related to
him, and even then it is not particularly well received.

At the gallery, I notice there are no round red stickers on any of the paintings, which means he hasn't sold anything. Oh, Matthew. I decide to buy something. I am a grown woman with a job in corporate America who has long since paid off her college loans, and I live in a cheap apartment and I have money in my savings account. I can buy a painting if I want. I pick a rendering of a dark pit that gives the illusion of peering directly into it. It's actually rather deft. At the bottom there's a tiny bright white circle. Life at the bottom of the pit. I hand my credit card over to the gallery owner. I am now a person who buys art, I think. Instead of making it.

Ten minutes later Matthew and I stand in front of the gallery, two lukewarm beer bottles in our hands. "You're looking good," he says. "You too," I say. We clink our bottles together in a bit of triumph. We are aging but not aged.

I ask him if he's excited about his show.

"Well, you're the only person who bought anything," he says. "Which should keep the lights on for about a month, so thank you very much. But just the apartment lights, not the studio lights, so I think I'm getting rid of my studio, whoops. Also my roommate moved out last weekend, and just the fact that I even have a roommate and I'm almost forty years old has its own set of problems. And I still haven't paid off grad school."

"But so many people came tonight," I say. "To *your* show."

"To gossip and drink free beer."

"I came to see just you and your art," I say. "This beer means nothing to me, do you hear me? Nothing."

"And that's why you're my favorite person in the whole world," he says, which is definitely not true, and then he kisses me. I don't think he knew he was going to do it or even why he did it, and he steps back after the kiss and his pupils look enormous, his eyes, also enormous, and he flaps his arms, and a little beer flies up in the air. The whole series of events catches me off guard. But I like feeling unsettled. So we sleep together.

And it's actually lovely, sweet, slow, 1970s, West Coast, beachy sex. All his parts are in working order and so are mine. He holds himself nearly motionless in me for long stretches of time and I lie there and breathe deeply and then he buries himself in my breasts and says, "Mmm." Then at the end he moves brusquely, and I like it. I shriek.

"You're so loud," he says, teasingly, when we are finished.

"That's because I'm in pain," I reply, without even thinking about it.

"Oh my god, was I hurting you?"

"No, I'm in pain here," I say, and pat my chest. "It's OK," I say. "I'm used to it."

Immediately he holds me.

His apartment is a wreck and his clothes are everywhere and there are paint flecks on the floor and dust on the bookshelves. Only for a moment do I consider how I would feel about this squalor over the long haul. Instead I find it a relief: I have my own kind of squalor. We're both grown up although not necessarily grown-ups, and I don't feel any pressure to be anything that I'm not.

I stay longer than I mean to in the morning because we end up having a nice conversation about his niece, who is an aspiring artist. "She's better than I was at her age," he says. He walks me to the train and we stop for coffee and he doesn't offer to pay for me and I find myself offering to pay for him instead. Why not? It costs so little it's almost like it doesn't cost anything at all. "Don't say I don't ever do anything nice for you," I tell him. "I didn't and I couldn't and I wouldn't," he says.

"Literally the most depressing thing I've ever seen in my life," says my coworker Nina, peering at an image of the painting on the gallery's website.

"There's a lot of interesting textures and layers to it," I say defensively. "You should see it up close."

"Pass." Then: "I'm not saying it's not *good*."

"Right," I say.

"I'm just saying it's depressing," she says.

The next week Matthew invites me over for dinner at his apartment. I text him and ask if I can bring anything. He texts back: "Just yourself." An hour later he texts me and asks if I can pick up a bottle of wine. Fifteen minutes later he texts: "And maybe some bread?" I bring an expensive bottle of Cabernet and an enormous loaf of sourdough bread, which I know we'll never be able to finish, so he'll have some for lunch the next day. I also bring a small bottle of bourbon and a round of goat cheese. And a bar of dark chocolate. All of these things I would want to eat and all of these things I know he will not have.

We eat everything I have brought and also power grains and vegetables from his CSA farm share. One of the vegetables is tough. We chew and chew. "What is this purple vegetable?" I say. He sighs. "I don't even know. I was just guessing on how to cook it. I was trying to use up the rest of my farm share. The recipe called for eggplant. I should have just bought an eggplant. I have no money right now, though." "I know you don't have any money," I say quietly. He stands abruptly and stalks to his freezer and swings it open dramatically. The freezer is crammed with Tupperware containers. He tells me he cooks whatever's left over every week and freezes it for later meals. "Thrifty," I say. "I am living on last month's vegetables," he says. "I can bring an eggplant," I say. "Next time, eggplant's on me." "Is this any way to live?" he says. "Come on, sit down," I say. "We were having such a nice meal."

I can't stand when a meal is ruined. I have slept with many men, don't ask me their names, but I can't eat anything casually. *Don't fuck with my food,* I want to say to him.

"Come here, baby," I say instead. I kiss him and he kisses me and we laugh and we are close and I believe so deeply in that moment that I can tolerate his bullshit. I tell him about my family when I was growing up, how my mother used to make us rice and beans and call it Mexican night and say we were having a fiesta and teach us Spanish words at the table and play flamenco albums. "But I promise you we were just eating rice and beans because we had no money in the bank," I say.

"You don't care?" he says.

"I don't care," I say.

"Then let's eat," he says.

We have sex instead, and it is even deeper and closer this time, as if he has crawled up inside my womb and nestled there for safety. I hold his face in my hands, and we look at each other and don't speak, and the room closes in on us, I feel it, the world is shrinking, and there is just him and me, physically connected, as close to being one as we can be. Gross.

In the morning, lazy, we talk to each other as friends, catching up on old times, years lost. Matthew asks me what happened when I left grad school. It's better than talking to anyone else about it, better than my therapist, better than any of my New York City friends, because he was there, even if he didn't know what happened.

"I didn't really understand it all," he says. "You were there and then you were gone."

"My mentor dumped me," I say. She broke my heart. It was not a man who sucked the life out of me. It was a woman.

"I remember her," he says. "She's still there. She never went anywhere but there."

"She's still great," I say, always protective of her, even as I carry an active wound she carved into me. "I saw one of her pieces in a group show last year."

"Well, I don't know about great," he says.

"What do you know?" I snap.

A few days later I am in a bad mood because I hate my job, my meaningless fucking job, and I meet him at a bar halfway between our apartments and we have a drink, well, three, and I barely manage not to be a cunt to him the entire night.

"Just because she dumped you doesn't mean you had to stop making art entirely," he says. "I could never give up painting, ever. I don't know what I would do without it."

Are we still talking about this? We are still talking about this.

"Because I didn't have it in me," I say. "The minute I felt unsupported I gave up. I saw that to be a painter meant a lifetime of not being supported."

"That's correct," he says. He's proud of himself for his capacity to handle rejection. He is comfortable living in the realm of failure and struggle.

"And I didn't want to feel that way," I say. "I have a hard enough time being me, not pulling myself apart every single day. And if it wasn't just my personality and my life choices, but then also my art too? I would die." I would probably be dead by now, I don't say, but I know that's true; I know how close I came to it then.

We hold hands in public. This is a thing now, the two of us.

I call my mother in New Hampshire, in the small town where she has been living for nine months with my brother and his wife and their sick baby, and I tell her I've started dating a man. "What's he like?" she asks. I give her the highlights: he's an artist, he's poor, he's kind, he's sensitive, when he's not feeling depressed he makes me feel good about myself. "You know who he sounds like?" says my mother. "Is there any way the answer to this is not my father?" I say. "Let's have a different conversation," says my mother.

"What do you want to talk about?" I say. My mother breathes through her nose, a deep, yogic breath. I've already taken one wrong turn in this conversation; it's on me to find a right turn. "How's New Hampshire?" I say. "Is your presence there helping at all?" "They're still fighting," she says. "Your brother is so quiet. I want to blame her for something, but it doesn't necessarily need to be anyone's fault. Sometimes things just go wrong." "How about the baby?" I say. "Can you help there?" "No one can help that baby," says my mother. "I help and I help and I help, and none of it makes a difference. She's going to die someday soon."

"Let's go back to talking about how I sleep with men that remind me of my father," I say. "I actually think that's a better conversation."

"I've got a better idea," says my mother. "Tell me about what you did today. Tell me about New York." So I do, I tell the lifelong New Yorker who chucked it for the woods about the streets of the city: how the subway was so crowded this morning I had to let four trains pass in a row and I was a half hour late to work; how I had a meeting in Times Square and I saw an army of painted topless women posing with tourists for money; how I saw two people dressed up as Disney characters get into a fistfight; how I ate a hot dog from a stand after my client meeting bombed and when I finished it I ate another, on one of the chairs scattered in Bryant Park. A string quartet was playing nearby, under a sponsor banner. "The music part was the part that saved me," I say. "All of it would have saved me," says my mother.

A few days after I talk to my mother, I am supposed to see Matthew at a dinner with my friend Indigo and her rich husband. I call her and say, "Indigo, please, can we go somewhere not insanely expensive because this guy has no money. Like, let's just go somewhere casual, do you know how to do casual anymore?" And then she reminds me that she grew up broke just like me, she is huffy about it, and it was in Trinidad part of the time, and Trinidad broke is way worse than Upper West Side broke, and she says she'll call me later to let me know where she's made the reservation, and then an hour later she texts me a picture of a McDonald's with the message "See you at 7!" And I text her back, "You're being fucked up," and she texts me back, "I know, I'm sorry, things aren't good over here right now," and I text, "Do you want to talk about it?" And she texts, "No." And then a few minutes later she texts, "I do, but not right now." A few minutes after that, she texts, "I'm sorry." Then she calls me and she's crying and we talk for a while about her marriage and while I am sad that my friend is sad, it makes me happier than ever that I've never been married and never will be, because marriage sounds like a goddamn job, and why would I want another one of those?

We skip dinner with Indigo and her husband. Instead I collapse onto Matthew's couch in his living room while he swivels around nervously on a chair. I tell him the whole story about Indigo's marriage and then I say, "See? Money doesn't make you happy." And he says, "Easy for you to say." "Now what?" I say. He pulls out his wallet, his hands weirdly shaking, and he removes a card: it says EBT on it. "Food stamps, it's that bad," he says.

Then I tell him a story about the first time my family went on food stamps. It was during winter break from school, and I saw the food stamps on the kitchen table and I didn't know what they were exactly; I thought maybe they were some sort of play money, like from Monopoly, a toy for me. I was eight, and my mother was ignoring me that day, probably because she was too worried about keeping us fed, and my father was not much help in the matter. I set to making an artful winter collage, shredded paper for icicles, miniature snowflake cutouts, the full display taped to the bathroom mirror. I made my mother cry, and then I started crying, and then there were the two of us holding each other in the bathroom crying, and she said, so sadly— oh, I can hear the tone of her voice even now!—to me, "I just need a little help." I tell Matthew this whole story a little proudly. Bad childhood stories are kind of my thing.

"I know that you are trying to make me feel better," he says, "but it's not working. Our tragedies are different. You are telling me the story of something that happened to you and I am telling you the story of something I did. I put myself here. In this hole."

That night we do not have sex but we sleep together, side by side, not touching, until he gives in and touches me first, and we kiss good night, hold hands for a while, and then pull apart again to our separate sides of the bed.

The honeymoon is over, I think. But at least it lasted longer than usual.

• • •

The next time I see Matthew I tell him I'm going to take him out to dinner. I'm hungry. "I don't want to hear it," I say. "I just want to eat." We order a nice meal, filet mignon, fried potatoes, creamed spinach, at a classic steakhouse in my neighborhood, with waiters in white button-down shirts and black pants and bow ties, chain-smoking, unsmiling foreigners who provide flawless service.

"This is very nice," he says quietly. "Isn't it?" I say. We salt our food furiously. He says not much else for the entire meal, except for this: "You have to know this is who I am." And I say, "I got it."

Later, in bed, I tell him, "Men are babies, but some of them have big, beautiful cocks." I put my hand on him, get it the way I like it, hard, a little moist at the tip. We have sex that feels great but is not particularly fun. I am treating him like something different than usual. I am treating him like everyone else.

"Is it possible you're scared?" says my therapist, her penciled-in eyebrows raised.

"It's possible," I say. "But maybe it's more that I grew up in a household where I watched my mother be oppressed first by my junkie father and then secondly by every loser stoner who walked through the door even though she was supposedly this strong independent smart woman who should have survived on her own, but felt like she was supposed to ask for help. And maybe because I didn't have any positive relationship models in my life I don't feel inspired to make concessions to keep this one, because what's the point, men will suck you dry anyway?"

"Now there you go, Andrea!" she says. "Nice work." And she pretends I've had this big breakthrough, but I've been saying this for years, I said it the first day I showed up in her office, once I stopped weeping.

What do you do when you already know what your problem is? What if it's not really a problem? It's only a problem if I want a relationship. If I want to fit into a conventional mode of happiness. It's only a problem if I care. And I can't tell if I care.

"I can't tell what you want," says my therapist.

"Neither can I," I say.

Then I turn forty. The first thing I do for my birthday is fire my therapist, who, after nearly a decade, I have determined is useless. Then I invite a bunch of people to dinner, a few friends from childhood and college who still live in the city, some neighbors from my apartment building, Indigo, and even my mother offers to come to town. No pressure, just everyone I know in one place. I include Matthew on the invite list, of course, because he is the man in my life and he says he'll come for a drink after, and I ask why he won't come to dinner, and he says, "You know why." I say, "It's fine, I'll pay," and he says, "You shouldn't have to pay, it's your birthday," and I say, "It's fine," and he says, "It's not fine," and I say, "All I want for my birthday is for you to not ruin another meal," and he says, "It's like that, is it?" And I say yes. Then we have an hourlong conversation about where we are at, and it goes from something nice enough to terrible in that hour, which is not what I thought was the reality but I guess it is now.

My birthday dinner is pleasant, if slightly forced. We dine in the candlelit basement of an Italian restaurant near my house. I have the porchetta and a thousand glasses of wine. Everyone manages to not talk about their own bullshit for a night, a real effort for some—Indigo with her bad marriage, my mother always worried about her family, an old drug buddy who keeps disappearing to the bathroom—and instead they say really nice things about me, that I am an honest and good friend, that I am strong and fair, that I have enviable hair, that I haven't aged a day. To that last bit I say, "That's because I've spent the last decade trapped in an office, the sun hasn't touched this skin!" Everyone laughs. Then they make jokes about me turning forty, but you know what, tonight I don't care about forty, joke away. To my great surprise I am still alive on this planet. And that's what we toast to—to still being alive.

My mother hugs me hard at the end of the night, hugs everyone hard; she is a little drunk, and also she has be-friended everyone at the table. I had hoped my brother would show up too, but no dice. He is lost to the wilds of

New Hampshire. And of course Matthew does not show up for a birthday drink.

"Too bad," says my coworker Nina. "It sounded like you really liked him."

"Too bad," says my mother. "I was looking forward to meeting him. It's been so long since you've introduced me to someone new."

A week later the phone rings and it's a local number, I don't recognize it, and I'm praying that it's Matthew calling me from some mysterious location to tell me he's missing me and thinking about me so that I don't have to call him and say it myself. But instead it's his gallery, calling to tell me I can pick up the painting of his I bought at his opening. I pick it up, but I'm no fool, I don't hang it. That's not how you get over someone, by looking at his artwork every day. I keep it wrapped in paper, in my closet, behind my winter boots. Someday when I'm dead, I think, people will find this hidden painting and wonder who was so depressed they could have made something like that.

A month passes and I realize I'm not thinking about him as much, just once or twice a day, and then another two weeks pass and I realize oh, I only thought about him a few times this week, and then another two weeks go by and I don't think about him once the entire time, and then another week after that it occurs to me that I am thinking about him constantly, and before I can talk myself out of it I call him and ask him to meet me for a drink, just as friends, my treat, and he says yes.

I see him every once in a while now. The fucking we did hangs between us, but we will not return to it. Better to deny desire than to collapse from it. I tell him he's my friend and I love him and he is a true artist and I admire him for doing what he's doing and he shouldn't second-guess, just let me pay the bill so he can eat. And he says, Really? And I tell him: Yes. It's nothing. I won't even remember it tomorrow. You eat like a bird. You should eat more. Let me feed you. Here you go. Take a bite. And another. That's a good boy.

FELICIA

An apartment in Chicago, April 2002. I sit at the feet of Felicia, the most famous instructor in our program. I am in her apartment in her Logan Square building, which she restored on her own. Like she took a book on home improvement out of the library, read it, and then just did the spackling and electrical wiring and tiling herself because it needed to be done. She dresses in all black, jeans, T-shirts, lacy see-through things sometimes, and she has an amazing body, sinewy, tough, tan arms and a tight ass, and long fairy-dust hair, blond-gray, which she wears in braids sometimes. Also she has incredible jewelry, the real stuff, diamonds and gold and platinum, most of it inherited from an affluent aunt who never had children of her own, although Felicia did apprentice with a jeweler for a while so some of it she made herself. She has three solo gallery shows in the next

year, one of them in Berlin, and has been commissioned to
do an installation in Brazil, where she basically was given
a town square to do with whatever she likes. Nothing she
owns comes from a man. Everything she touches turns into
something bigger. She has made herself out of scratch. I am
twenty-six and I would cut off my left tit to be her.

I am not alone at her feet. There is her boyfriend, twenty
years younger. Josiah, escaped from a rainbow cult as a
teen, brutally gorgeous, tall, and muscular, a welder, incredible arms. All his clothes seem to hover around his body,
barely attached. Spiky hair, big lips, combat boots. My groin
toils now just thinking about him.

Felicia is ranting. The Germans are being demanding.
They're fucked up in both their requirements and tone. It's
not that it's daunting her, it's just *distressing*. And she hates
her students: demanding too, though differently than the
Germans, always wanting her approval, needing her love,
when they should just focus on their art instead. Also there's
a burst pipe and a canceled flight. Fifty things at once. I
worry urgently about being one of the needy students. I
want to ask her if that's how she thinks of me. I crave it like
I crave a drink. But instead I say, "Felicia, let me help you,"
because that is my job.

I am her assistant on various projects, plucked from the
crowd because I am smart and efficient but also a good time,
young and flirty and boozy. I go wherever she wants me to
go and I tell her she's perfect without her having to ask. I met

her at a party in September, at the beginning of the school year. From my seat on the sunken couch I watched her that night with another young woman, a big-eyed blonde, tall, a student from Denmark, in the corner, Felicia's hands on her shoulders. The student was drunk, and not handling whatever was happening well. She collapsed a bit; she was sloppy. I rose from the couch to help. Together we dumped the blonde into a cab. "You," said Felicia, a little drunk herself. "You I like." Me. Later I find out the Danish student was Josiah's ex-girlfriend. She returned from whence she came a month later.

I begin to skip classes whenever Felicia calls me. I don't even think to say no. Studio time, reading the things I need to read, contemplating my critiques—I am unconcerned with all of this. For the past decade of my life I had painted, blindly. La Guardia for four years, and then a small scholarship sent me to Hunter. Waiting tables, smelling fumes. It was the only thing I knew to do with my time besides drink and eat and screw. It kept me company. And now here was this woman suggesting I spend time with her instead. She would be my company.

Across town, I hate my roommate, this twenty-two-year-old rich bitch from Winnetka, who thinks she's slumming because she's living with an artist. It's her apartment, meaning she owns it because her parents bought it for her, and she rents out the extra room. She basically doesn't have a job. She gets weekly manicures. She says "Ta" instead of

"Thank you" because she spent a year abroad in England. Also she has a lover, a married lawyer, one of her father's friends, and he fucks and leaves, sometimes before the dinner hour is over. Like I'm eating dinner and they're having sex in the other room. He has children. "It's a secret," she says to me giddily. "You can't tell anyone." You don't have anything to worry about, I tell her. Because I don't care about your secrets. It doesn't take much of a push for me to want to spend all my time with Felicia.

In November, one night, upon finishing a second bottle of wine with Felicia:

I'll tell you a secret.

Tell me.

I don't think any of you have talent. I'm just trying to pay my bills.

You don't think that, I say. You're kidding, right. Please tell me you're kidding, Felicia.

I grab her arm.

I'm just kidding, she says. *I'm just messing with you.*

I become more interested in her work than in my work. Her projects feel innovative and important. My paintings feel basic and insignificant. In truth, they are. I have a good sense of humor and there's a cleverness to my work and I understand color and I know how to choose interesting subject matter, real-life people, places, things, and before I got to grad school I had the necessary discipline, but I wonder, daily, if I have enough hunger. To be an artist means a lifetime of being told no, with the occasional yes showing up just to give you enough hope to carry on. I am beginning to realize I don't want to be rejected my entire life. Felicia has never accepted the rejection, though. Felicia is always hustling. Felicia spits on your no. If I stay with her long enough will I learn how to be like Felicia? I swirl my whiskey, I drink my beer, I write in my notebook, I think about Felicia.

Another night in November:

But do you think I have what it takes?

You're nascent, you're a baby, you're a puppy. Don't worry, just do your work. You're on your way.

We work hard all day. Josiah is devoted to Felicia, obsessed with her projects, but with his own art, too. In my memory he appears as someone who is constantly lifting heavy objects. Meanwhile, Felicia's on the phone at all hours. Time zones have destroyed her life. No one is sleeping. The air is tense and full and exciting. I have convinced myself I am learning far more by spending time with Felicia than listening to lectures, which is probably not inaccurate. I am still painting, though. I go early in the mornings and I stare at the blank canvas until it is full. Staring and painting. Trying to figure something out. Did I have what it took? Did I belong there? Why did she even like me? I abandoned those paintings when I left town so I'll never know if they were any good. But I think they were all right. They weren't bad, those paintings. Doesn't matter anyway—they're lost now.

In December my mother runs out of money. Her lights are shut off for one weekend, and she can't pay her rent. Her new boyfriend has been covering all the bills while she works for another low-paying nonprofit. He hits her, just once, but no fool my mother, she knows once is enough, once always leads to twice, and he's out of her apartment immediately, his things waiting for him on the street when he returns from a night in jail. I send her a check so she can pay her rent for a few months. My brother and his girlfriend offer to foot the bill for her expensive therapist. I don't think about how I'll pay my own rent, but by Christmas I realize I'm broke myself. I tell Felicia. I don't tell her why. I don't want her to know about the weakness of my own mother. I let her think I'm the fool instead.

With great enthusiasm we agree I should move into the Logan Square apartment, at least for the spring semester. What a terrible idea. I mean, whose idea was it, anyway? I really want to remember but I can't. It was dumb, but I wanted to be there, with the two of them, not for any reason other than I enjoyed the closeness we all had. "It'll be nice to have you around," says Felicia. "I like a full house." This last bit is so charming. It's almost as if she's admitting a weakness, a loneliness like the rest of us have. I like seeing it but also I am torn, because I liked the idea of her not needing me too, not needing anyone at all, because that was perhaps the thing that impressed me most of all about her.

I fully stop going to classes, my dirty little secret, but surely she must know, because I am nearly always around the apartment, hiding from the Chicago winter, dashing out only for more liquor supplies, wearing three sweaters and two scarves and long johns. The booze keeping me warm, keeping us all warm.

I can hear them in the night. I see him in the morning, shirtless. It is hard not to look at Josiah shirtless. I admire his beauty, but I don't desire him then; I only desire him in retrospect, now, as a forty-year-old woman. Still, I'm sure she catches me looking. But how could I ever explain to her, though, that she was the one I loved?

Felicia, in the morning, on a phone interview:

I traffic in the real. How can you ignore what's right in front of your face?

Felicia, over my shoulder, looking at my work on her work:

Close, but not quite.

At the end of February, on a Friday night, she starts a fight with Josiah for no reason and he's not fighting back and it reminds me of my childhood, not the particulars of the dynamic, just, hazily, Mom and Dad fighting.

I leave the apartment. I go to a student party, and there I meet a man named Christopher, a watery-eyed sculptor with incredible bushy eyebrows, and I go home with him and we have breakfast together the next morning in a diner, fried eggs and toast with butter and jelly and orange juice made from concentrate and all the coffee in the world, and I hug him goodbye on the street and he asks me for my number and I tell him, "I don't have one," which is true. And then the next night I go out drinking in Wicker Park and I meet another man, sort of a grown-up guy with a real job, and we get extremely drunk and I go home with him and he tries to get me to give him a blowjob, not overly insistently but it's still annoying, like just drop it already, buddy, I get that it's your favorite thing in the world but it's not *my* favorite thing in the world, and so I fake pass out until I actually do. His apartment is huge with high windows that face the street and in the morning the sunlight wakes me, and it's deceptive, this sun, because I know outside it's a bitter cold Chicago winter morning. I sneak naked across the apartment, the floors are freezing, and I shudder as I dress. When I walk outside the snow is dirty and I put my hand to my eyes. I have no idea where I am.

Eventually I find the Brown Line but I get on it in the wrong direction, and I don't realize it for a few stops and then by the time I do it's just easier to transfer to another line to get home, but then that train ends two stops before the one I need because of track construction. I think: Why am I being punished? Finally I arrive at Felicia's, and silently we work together, both of us ignoring the fight I had witnessed a few days before, and my ensuing disappearance. I puke once in the afternoon and then that night I go to another student party, and I run into my friend Matthew, a sad-faced scarecrow, jittery, talented, incredibly sweet, and he feels suddenly like the only person on the planet I can talk to, so I go home with him and that feels good, I just collapse for a while, and he doesn't want much from me, he just lets me be, and so I just sit.

My mother's birthday is in mid-March, and I call her for the first time in two months and she says, "All I want for my birthday is for you to come home." Which is strange because my mother is not an extraordinarily needy person when it comes to me. I wasn't even sure she would notice I had moved to Chicago. And I say, "Mom, have you been taking your meds?" and she says, "What are you talking about, I don't take medication," and I say, "Oh, you just sounded like you needed some for a second," and she says, "Why can't you just say happy birthday to me like a normal person?" Then she hangs up on me. I couldn't even be nice to my mother on her birthday. I am sorry now that I was so selfish then but I swear I was hanging on for dear life.

And now it's the end of April, and Felicia's upset about every single thing in her life. I'm on the floor, cross-legged, imitating calm, while Felicia stands above me complaining. The show, the Germans, the pipes, the plane, the students. She ignores my offer of assistance. Josiah and I exchange the lightest of glances, pointedly insignificant, but where else would I look? He was the only other person in the room not yelling. I think: Help me, tell me how to become a person she'll love. I'll never know what he was thinking, because Josiah was unknowable to me. When I look up at Felicia, she is twisting her head back and forth between us. I see on her face a presumption being formed. Josiah, across the room, also seated on the floor, suggests they take a walk together, she and him. "You take a walk," she says. "The two of you. I can't look at either of you." She points toward the door. "Go." I bend forward like an animal and make my way up awkwardly. Josiah crouches and then rises, lightning quick. Together we leave.

"We should probably drink something," I say.

We go to a bar a few blocks away: fluorescent Old Style sign in the window, jukebox half indie rock, half blues, pool table, dartboards, Polish men. We order whiskey and beer. I eat every pretzel in the bowl and ask for another. I want him to tell me the truth, though about what, I do not know.

He tells me about his childhood, growing up in the cult. Intense day-, week-, and month-long Bible study sessions. Running out of money, often. Starving, often. A beautiful child, hair down to his waist. The father who freed him

when he was fifteen. Family members spread across South
America. The true-believer mother whom he alternately
loathes and loves.

"I talk to her once a year on her birthday," he says. "And
even after everything, she always asks when I'm coming
home."

"I know that song," I say.

"You think Felicia is tough but I've seen worse," he says.

"I didn't say Felicia was tough," I say.

"I did," he says, and we both laugh, and it is nice we
are laughing, though I don't think it's about quite the same
thing.

We go home, toasted, noisy, wired but still calmer than
before. The house is empty, who knows where Felicia went?
This is a trap, I think. Do not even hug him good night. I
go to my room, by myself, proudly. Look at you, doing the
right thing, I think. Look at you not sleeping with the wrong
man for once.

But I might as well have done it, scaled him, straddled
him, slid between his sheets. Because a glance is as mean-
ingful as a fuck. There is Felicia at three a.m., drunk, knocking on the guest room door, soft, laughing, cursing, then
loud, rude, sneering, saying things I can't understand, until
finally she opens the door and I hear one hissed, hovering
word: *Quit.*

The next day I leave. I take a train back to New York. My
brother is having a housewarming party; he and his smart,

pretty, stable, magazine editor girlfriend have moved in together. All of his band members are there, and I very pub-
licly and drunkenly pick one up and leave the party with
him because apparently I want to destroy *everything*. I bum
around the city with him for a few days, until we tire of
each other. In his bedroom, desperate, I call my mother.

"I heard you're a mess," my mother says to me.

"I heard *you're* a mess," I snap.

She sighs. "You can still come home," she says. "You can
always come home."

But I don't want to live in New York, not yet. I go back
to Chicago instead. It's May, and my MFA program would
like to know what my intentions are. I show up at Matthew's apartment one day and stay. I mention nothing
about my life, my truth, my reality. He allows me to curl
up into him, and he holds me steady while I breathe. Neither of us leaves for days. He can't stop working, though, so
he continues to paint at home. His apartment reeks of tur-
pentine and I watch him one morning while he's working
and he has this very specific and peaceful look on his face
and I feel extreme envy because this is not how I feel about
my own work and at that exact moment I realize I don't
know what I'm doing with my life but I know I don't want
to paint any longer. The next morning I sneak out of Matthew's house and get on another train and I take it all the
way home to New York City. I stop painting entirely. I get a
job in advertising. I get older. I grow up, I suppose. I never

look back except in those moments when I can't stop fucking thinking about it.

I can tell you something remarkable about that time, although it has only just occurred to me now. I never thought about death, like I do now. I never worried about dying. I only ever thought about being alive.

BETSY

My mother's friend Betsy, the old radical, dies after a short illness. Pneumonia, sepsis, done. "I hope I go that fast," says my mother. "Let's not talk about you dying," I say, although I agree with her, both for her sake and mine. There's a small, vaguely illegal funeral, involving Betsy's ashes and sneaking onto a dock under a full moon at midnight on Sheepshead Bay. My mother elects not to attend it. "I'm too old to jump fences," she says. No one is arrested, she later reports. A few weeks after that, there is a public memorial service in the city, at which my mother has been asked to speak. She invites me to join her. The only other memorial service I have been to in my life is my father's, twenty-five years ago. "When you get older you go to things like this all the time," says my mother. "Something to really look forward to," I say. "Well, at least you're not the one who's dead," says my mother.

I skip work, which I have been doing a lot lately. A bereavement day, I say to my boss, who cannot, try as he might, argue with death. He has nearly given up on me, nearly, nearly, and yet the thought of hiring someone new to do a job I have done extremely well for a decade troubles him. How would he remove everything in my brain and put it in someone else's? And my absences do not seem to affect my work, in part because I can do it blindfolded by now. Whatever thrill I had in perfecting my job is now dead, because perfection itself is boring; it's only everything leading up to it that's interesting.

"Did you finish . . ." my boss says.

Yes, everything is done. Everything is always done.

He taps a pen on his desk and then remembers how to behave in this particular scenario. "I'm sorry for your loss," he says.

"It's more for my mother," I say. "She was her best friend. Her name was Betsy. She was kind of her hero." "Hero" isn't right exactly, but I can't figure out a way to explain the nuances of their relationship. They were best friends, but Betsy was older. Betsy ran the show a little bit.

"I'm sorry for your mother's loss, then," he says.

"You know who the real loser here is?" I say. "Betsy."

Our throats fill with laughter and then we both make weird, funny faces, like faux-disgusted, shocked at our mutual inappropriateness, but this brings us closer together, too. Six years is a long time to know someone, though I don't know much more about him than when he started here, hired as a peer, now my boss. A wife framed in a picture, a boat, a house, a tennis racket in the summer, skis in the winter, Scotch at the holiday party. We're the same age and he possesses much more than I ever will. But at least I don't have to be the boss of someone like me.

"Off you go," he says.

Betsy's memorial service is being held at St. Mark's Church. I haven't been there since high school, when I used to go to the New Year's Day marathon poetry readings, first with my family when my father was still alive, and later with a boy I'd met at the Empire State Building during a field trip. He went to a faraway magnet school in Brooklyn. We held hands in the pew while Patti Smith sang and played stridently, her long hair captured beneath her guitar strap. Then we got hot chocolate and wandered around Tompkins Square Park in the cold, huddled on a bench in the center of the park, and kissed a few times. After that day we disappeared from each other's lives, no fault of his or mine; we just lived so far away from each other. His name was Carlos. Where is he now? I should look him up on Facebook. Never mind, he's probably married anyway.

It's hot in the church. There are enormous industrial fans blowing in the vestibule and in the rear of the sanctuary itself, on a row of platform seats. Rickety, stained-glass

Jesuses all around. I spot my mother, who is surrounded by men. After my father died, she was always surrounded by men. She used to throw these drunken, druggy dinner parties. They swarmed her, I'll never quite understand why. A penniless widow with two children, in her forties, what a catch. But there they were, and here they are, though everyone is much older now.

These men had swarmed me, too, and that part I understood. I was a depressed teenage girl, a sitting duck with brand-new tits. I had made the men hazy in my mind, and now, looking out at this room, I could not tell you who had done what exactly. It was nothing in particular, other than coming home on a Saturday night, just a girl, a teenager, to a smoky, jazzy apartment full of people. My mother somewhere in there, laughing, a vague wave hello. I remember being pulled onto a lap and tickled, the pressure of a grown man's cock behind me, not on my skin, but on my clothes, and having to wiggle my way free. I never liked it, I never wanted it. I'd like to see them try the same thing now, I tell myself, a rush of aggression surging in me, suddenly prepared for physical violence. These frail old men. I'd bury them.

"Andrea, over here," says my mother, and the men scatter. An embrace, and I refuse to let her go, even though my current of rage extends to her. But I used to see her every Saturday and now I've seen her only once since she moved to New Hampshire. I've missed her. As per usual, I am having a hundred feelings at once.

I ask about David and Greta. "What do you want to know?" she asks. "I don't know," I say. I have a pretty good sense of what's going on with them, but I could be surprised. "Are they happy at all, ever?" "No," my mother says. "I don't know if they'll survive this." "That's terrible," I say. "It's a difficult situation, obviously. And I know you don't know this yet, but marriage all by itself is hard anyway," she says and examines a lock of my hair with concern. Can you believe this woman? She just says shit like that casually, with no regard, and then pretends my hair is the problem.

"Mom, just because I don't care about being married myself doesn't mean I don't understand how it works for other people."

"You're still young, you should care," she says. She studies the ends of my hair again. "But not so young that you don't have to take vitamins," she says, and then the memorial service begins.

There is a preamble from a niece. She loved Betsy. Betsy and her at the museums. Betsy taking her to her first protest. Betsy knitting her sweaters every year to keep her warm. Betsy as a nurturer, always lingering nearby, except when she wasn't, when she was traveling the world, which she was allowed to do, of course. Because Betsy was nobody's mother. "She went to China just last year," my mother tells me. "With a socialist tour group. She loved it."

Next: A tightly wrought man with the intensity of a squirrel, hands coiled, ponytailed, wearing a denim jacket and a neatly buttoned up shirt tucked into khaki pants. He clutches a stack of papers in his fist.

"Oh brother," says my mother. "Who is that?" I say. "Corbin. Betsy's first husband," she says.

A speech follows regarding the CIA, conspiracies, corruption, assassinations, various presidents, the contemporary state of activism, spy technology, Facebook, and Betsy's grit and determination to help this speaker reveal the truth, which is still being revealed, will always be being revealed, look around now, keep your eyes open, wake up and stay awake. Corbin concludes with: "And they'll never make another Betsy."

"Riveting," I say to my mother. "He was always a lunatic," she says. "I mean he's right about all that happening with the CIA, but still he was insane."

Across the room, in the front pew, a man in a wrinkled, oversized linen suit is staring at me, an older man with a tight goatee and a ponytail the color of rotting lemons. He's one of my mother's friends from before, when she had her parties. *He's a bad man,* I think. That's all I can remember. Bad man.

Betsy's second ex-husband, Morty, takes the stage. He openly weeps throughout his speech. "Too soon, too soon," he begins, and the crowd murmurs. She was there for him, like no one else. The tragedy of his life was losing her as his wife; the blessing of his life was that she remained his friend. *Good start,* I think. Then Morty goes on to detail three separate battles with cancer, near death twice, full recovery each time, the loss of his father, the loss of his mother, financial woes that fortunately turned to triumphs, but still, there was struggle there, and all that time, there was Betsy, supporting him. "Thank God for Betsy," he says, and then he's finished.

"He screwed half his cancer nurses is the thing he doesn't mention," says my mother. "Why was he even allowed to speak, then?" I ask her. "Who do you think paid her bills all those years while she was marching and volunteering?" my mother says. "He wrote big checks to whatever cause she wanted." I look up at Morty, who stumbles a bit as he leaves the podium. Several men in the front row rise to help keep him erect. "Morty is a terrible man," says my mother. "But Morty has *paid*."

The man in the front pew is still staring at me. God, he's got to be seventy by now, or maybe eighty? What was his name. Philip, Frederick, Foster, Felix. Felix, that's it. I will fuck you up, Felix.

Now taking the podium is Betsy's third ex, a woman named Deborah, gray-haired, bespectacled, wearing a witchy black dress with a smattering of black sequins, a delicious bosom, you just want to crawl up inside of it already. "She's very active in her temple and is furious this isn't being held there right now," whispers my mother. "But Betsy loved this church. And they weren't together for so long anyway. She has no rights here." Deborah says the

Kaddish. Gentle tears wind down her face. Deborah holds the room. I cry too.

Betsy was solid. She always came to help clean up the day after the parties, even though she never actually attended them. "Ech, I'd rather stay in," Betsy used to say. "Maybe the first hour of a party is interesting. Everything after that is just repetitive." After both my high school and college graduations she handed me a nice check. I was welcome at her house for Thanksgiving for life. She was seemingly always baking something, then dropping off a tin of it at our house. Her hair in two gray braids, her belly a comfort to be held up against, her scent of weed and sandalwood and sweet, crusted sugar.

And now it's finally time for my mother to speak. Blue-eyed, cropped salt-and-pepper hair, trim, wise, sexy, my mother cuts a fine figure. "Let me tell you about Betsy," she begins. She was just her friend, nothing more than that, not blood, not a spouse. "But we knew each other forty years, and we ran deep." She talks about how Betsy helped her through her own losses, and those of others, too, although she manages to do this without discussing a single specific event. She says Betsy was a role model, yes. She worried about other people more than herself. She worried endlessly about social justice and the state of the world and she acted on those concerns. But she also was a good time. She was funny, says my mother. She had a dry wit. She was the person you'd want standing next to you at a party. My mother quotes Alice Roosevelt Longworth: "If you can't say something good about someone, sit right here by me." My mother pauses, and then lands the punch line: "I wish Betsy were here right now, sitting next to me, because she'd have something to say about all of you." Everyone laughs. "She loved a lot—three marriages, oy vey!—and I believe she loved each person deeply." She stops and makes eye contact with the three ex-spouses. "She showed up in your lives when you needed her most." My mother nearly says something else, and then, disappointingly, doesn't. "But she was also happy on her own. She was happy in her own skin. And that was what I learned the most from her. How to live with myself."

There is relief in the room. People applaud the speech. This seems inappropriate, but my mother really nailed it. I feel giddy on her behalf.

I can't believe there is more to the service, that anyone would want to follow that act. But: A jazz band plays, a woman sings. A few more family members speak. And then, at last, it is time to eat. Everyone rises and I see Felix get up, leaning heavily on a cane. I could kick it out beneath him, a collapse, rubble, a pile of Felix. But I simply watch him hobble out the door, bidding no one goodbye. I don't even know if he's really who I think he is. He may be a ghost of all of them. All of these men.

We make our way to a reception room behind the sanctuary. There are trays of smoked salmon everywhere, mounds of it, with rye bread and capers and onions, and tiny, eggy snacks, pastries and quiches, and slim slices of prosciutto, rolled, and glistening pearls of mozzarella. A small bar in the corner serves rosé and Chardonnay, and some sort of amber hard liquor looms on a back table. I can't decide what to do first, eat or drink. I have been thirsty since I was a teenager, but where I come from, my bloodline, possesses hundreds of years of hunger. "Don't sleep on the whitefish salad," says my mother. "It's gorgeous."

We pile our plates liberally with food, then we lean against a back wall, a window above us, sunlight and shadows crisscrossing the room. "Good spread," I say. "Of course," says my mother. "I think Morty took care of it." "I'm sure it wasn't Corbin," I say. "Corbin is a joke," says my mother. "Morty might be a baby, but at least he had his act together." "Do you even like men?" I say. "I don't know," says my mother. "Sometimes?" "Same," I say.

My mother made it through, I suddenly realize. She didn't do it all on her own, though who does? But the act of watching her watch these men, her being with me, in our own little corner, thrills me. God, what if I just forgave her? What if I was just done, too? What if I was fine with myself? What if I made it through? And then I think: I'm so glad I fired my therapist. I got this all on my own.

We go back for seconds, without acknowledging any sense of gluttony. After a while she says, "I liked your father." "I know, he was the best. I mean he was absolutely the worst, but he was so much fun," I say. "Sure he was fun. He was on drugs," she says. Finally I decide to get a drink. "Me too, me too," says my mother.

One and a half glasses in, a man approaches us and asks my mother quite seriously if she'll speak at his funeral. My mother clutches at him and says, "Oh my god, are you sick?" and he says, "No, but you did such a nice job, I thought I'd make a reservation in advance." It quickly becomes the joke of the party, people asking my mother to speak at their own funeral. People she knows, people she doesn't know. "What a celebrity you are," I say, as a man with whitefish salad on his cheek meanders off. "Fans everywhere."

"Can you believe I spent so much time with these goons?" she says. "Except for Larry."

We watch Larry, a divorce lawyer with strong leftist tendencies, tall, bald, sun-kissed, funny, his laughter booming, holding hands with his not-so-new wife. They're up from Philadelphia.

"He is lovely," I admit.

"Larry's the one who got away," my mother muses.

His wife is wearing a sleeveless pink blouse, and her arms are freckled and toned. She used to own a dance studio.

"She's a widow, too," says my mother. "Only her husband was rich. And she didn't have any children."

"Surely you are not blaming your failure to secure Larry's affections on my existence," I say.

"No. It was all my own fault. I wasted time on these men. And now they seem like ghosts to me."

I drain the rest of my glass. "I forgive you, Mom," I say, but of course by saying this I am not forgiving her at all, because I'm bringing it up, I'm starting a little shitstorm, it's pure patented passive aggression. Anyway, it's too late now. Here we go.

"For what?"

"For everything from when I was a kid. With these men."

"You forgive me. OK, child."

She guzzles her wine, then laughs wildly.

"Look, you had it easier than me," she says. "You think Nana and Papa were busy supporting women's rights? No, they wanted me to meet a nice man and get married and cook and clean for him and give them grandchildren, and that's it. You were born into a world where feminism existed and was readily available to you. I had to acquire that knowledge. I didn't know I could be on my own."

"You still bug me about marriage all the time. You just did it forty-five minutes ago."

"I want you to have a copilot, that's all," she says. "Marriage is hard but I still think it would make things easier for you. It might make you happier."

"Betsy was married three times and in the end she died all by herself, quite happily. She was better off without those people. You were the one who loved her best, Mom."

"It's just nice to have something to believe in," she says. "Marriage is a beautiful idea."

"But why can't you just believe in me?" I say.

This is when my mother starts to cry. I haven't seen her cry since my father died and even then she was so pissed off at him for overdosing that it wasn't pure, there was too much anger mixed in there for her to get it all out properly. But this is her weeping, and this is me holding her. "I'm sorry your friend died," I say. I let her sob into me.

"I'm only in town for the day," she says. "Can we just love each other?"

I agree to it. I agree to love.

She goes off to get us more food, and I cross the room to the bar. In the corner I see Larry slow-dancing with his wife for a second. One arm up, the other around her waist. Two Jews, nuzzling quietly in the back room of a church. Still alive, still in love. The two of them together, a beautiful idea.

THE
DINNER PARTY

The year of all the dinner parties is 1992. I am seventeen years old, and my father has been dead for two years. After he passed away, we ran through what little savings we had in a few months. Forget about my mother making more money at her job, those grassroots organizations had nothing to spare. A small token raise, we're sorry for your loss. My mother starts throwing these rent-raising dinner parties to make a little extra cash. All-you-can-eat vegetarian food and boxed wine. The only people who come are a bunch of middle-aged stoner men. Sometimes these men will bring her gifts, fancy comestibles or wine or weed, on top of the ten dollars they paid to eat her food. It's her way of keeping things going.

My mother throws these parties on alternate Saturday nights in our apartment on the Upper West Side. A few of the men are disgusting. They keep pulling me onto their laps, bouncing me on their knees, only I'm no kid and they know it. Maybe one man is the worst out of all of them, with his dirty ponytail and stiff, wiry goatee. He leaves his hands on my hips for too long. *As if,* I say as I pull myself off his lap. I can do better than some gross old man.

So after a few of these parties I start to make plans to be out of the house the entire evening. I help my mother cook, I share a glass of wine with her best friend Betsy while Betsy smokes a cigarette out the kitchen window, and then I go, I'm gone, and I do not return until the next day. I see shows at CBGB and go to raves in Brooklyn and I hang out in Washington Square Park until it gets too late and scary. Sometimes I go to see my brother's band. I listen to records with my friends in their tiny bedrooms until their parents tell us to go to sleep. I like Nirvana and Hole and David Bowie and Pink Floyd and My Bloody Valentine and Public Enemy and A Tribe Called Quest. I listen to tons and tons of Mozart, in particular when I'm painting, because my father the musician had told me Mozart was good for the brain. I dream about living in Seattle or London or Los Angeles, but I would never leave New York, because there is no better city in the world. This last part I firmly believe, even though I have never been anywhere else.

One night, I go to the midnight showing of *The Rocky Horror Picture Show* in the East Village. My friends Asha and Jack go with me and we spend all our money on cans of

Jolt cola, which we mix with rum that Jack bought at the liquor store on 10th Street that also sold dime bags of so-so weed and absolutely terrible coke, which half the time was cut with baby laxative. Sometimes we had Jolt and sometimes we had bad coke and sometimes we had OK speed, which Jack got from his older boyfriends. It didn't matter to me one way or another. This was my way of keeping things going. And now I was going.

On the train home, Asha and Jack sit across from me, kissing, and it's dumb because they're both gay.

"Why are you guys making out?" I say.

"I don't know, something to do," says Jack slyly.

I don't want to go home because of the party but no one else's home was much better. Either there's a bad parent or no room. At Asha's house I'd have to sleep in the same bed as her and she always wanted to spoon and I didn't always feel like it because it meant more to her than it did to me. "I love your hair," she'd say, and sniff it and wrap it around her wrist. My hair is long, and wild, and huge. I couldn't stand the pressure.

Sleeping in the same bed as my friends used to be something innocent, and now all of a sudden it's not. Not when there are so many newly alert nerve endings. Not when the brain always click-click-clicks late at night, even when I'm alone. There is no such thing as the sleep of the innocent anymore.

"If you're trying to make me jealous, it won't work," I say to Asha and Jack on the train.

"We don't care what you think anyway," says Asha. "We're just making ourselves feel good."

"This is so stupid," I say. I care a little bit, but not in the way they think. They were just ignoring me; that's what I hate.

They start getting really into it, putting their hands all over each other, shoving their tongues in each other's mouths really deep. Asha makes an exaggerated moan. It starts to gross me out.

"Fuck this, I'm out," I say, and I jump off at 86th Street before they can say anything. I wave goodbye to them through the window as the train moves out of the station.

Now I'm alone on the street, and I've got fifteen blocks to walk. I take Broadway because it's the best lit, the most chance of running into other people, but it's three a.m., and it's uptown, and contrary to popular belief, the city does sleep sometimes.

Right around 92nd Street, I pass a man, not a kid, definitely a man, drunk, holding a 40 in a paper bag. He offers me some. I say, "No thanks." I walk faster. He follows me and says, "How about you buy me another?" I say, "I don't have any money," and he says, "Yeah, right," and I say, "I'm broke, I'm probably broker than you are," and he says, "Who says I'm broke, why you think I'm broke, maybe

I just want your money anyway," and I start running now, why not run, why stand still just to prove some point? I have zero points. I hear glass break behind me and he's running too, I can hear him breathing heavy, he's a big guy, longer legs, but I'm pretty fast, I scored high in the Presidential Fitness Test at school, speed and flexibility, those are my strong suits, but no strength, so there's no way I'd win this fight. Don't stop, I tell myself. He is a man but you are a girl and you are on fire. Run all the way home. But then I feel a hand on my shoulder and I stumble and then somehow, just nearly, I escape his fingers, but I'm at the corner of West End Avenue, I run into a red light, and then a cab stops short in front of me, honks at me, honks at him, there's a light rain, I now notice, a sheen on me and the cab, and the wipers are going, and the man is gone. "Motherfucker," I exhale. I wave at the cabdriver. I mouth thanks. He doesn't know why I'm thanking him. He honks again.

Six more blocks and I'm home. I run the whole way. We live in a tall apartment building, no doorman, pretty clean, and, most important, rent-stabilized. It was my father's place first, and his aunt's before that. "It was the best thing I got out of this marriage," my mother was fond of saying, ignoring the fact that, hey, there were two kids who came out of it, too. It has a dining room and a small sunken living room with two big windows so the room is bright during the day. The kitchen has a black-and-white-tile floor and pots and pans hanging everywhere from hooks my father installed and a radiator that steams up the window. There are three bedrooms, each with its own closet, and windows facing a back alley, and also there is one bathroom with pink tiles and an enormous claw-foot bathtub, where I take long baths after school every day and read. Even though we have no money, this apartment makes us rich, because we were not crawling all over each other like a lot of other people in New York City, not to mention the rest of world where people live in huts and tents or nowhere in particular at all. A door you can close for privacy and sunlight sneaking through a back alley: forget it, we were millionaires.

But my home has changed since my mother started throwing the parties. Coming out of the elevator I can already smell the pot down the hallway. This new phase of drug usage in my home makes me miss the days when my father was just a heroin addict. Things were bad but at least you couldn't smell it from a mile away.

What I'd like to do when I walk in the front door is cry in my mother's arms, but I know I can't, because the minute I admit I'm not safe out there on my own I'll be forced to stay in on the weekends. So instead I breeze through the living room, where half a dozen men are stretched out, on the rug, on the couch, on a black lounger. They're graying, bearded, balding, the beginnings of potbellies on some, all this aging in process before me. Are they all a hundred years old? Was my father this old? My mother is sitting on the floor, her back perched up against the couch, and all I see is a head on her lap, a body presumably stretched out next to her, the rest of him hidden behind a long, low table. Here it is, the remains of a dinner party.

They all say my name, delighted, a change of scenery. Youth before them. "How was your night?" asks my mother. She straightens herself. Her blouse is loose. She is not naked but she is certainly not dressed either. *Is this your idea of fun* is a thing I always want to ask her. *Is this what I have to look forward to someday?* "Same as always," I say. I am furious with her. I had been tamping it down all night and now my anger is a brilliant, pulsing red, fully blossomed. "I'm going to bed." "No, stay up and talk to us," says one man, some loser. "Tell us what's going on with the kids today."

A thing I know now as an adult is this: there is no one cooler than a teenager. Even at our worst, our eyes are so fresh, and we have just enough knowledge to approach the world with a level of sophistication. People who say they didn't get cool till college or their twenties or whatever are incorrect. After our teenage years the game is over and we're all just holding on till death. And it is because I am at my peak cool, I know I am better than all these men.

How do I get all of these people out of my house? I decide to clean. Loudly. I clear the table, bowls with limp collards on top of saffron rice, stubbed-out cigarettes and joints in one bowl, the designated ashtray, half an enormous kale and radish salad left—tomorrow's lunch, I guess—and some sort of tofu bean sauce bullshit, and one whole fish carcass, gutted, picked apart, a limp banana leaf nearby. I clang and clink. I move fast. A few wedges of expensive-looking cheese, melting but not melted, holding on for dear life, lay on a cutting board. I wrap those up and hide them in the crisper. That's my cheese, I think. There's not much left that's appealing to me, but food is food, and the cupboards are often bare in our house, so I box it all up in Tupperware.

When I am done, the fridge looks full. This is a comforting feeling. Before my father died, we did not live abundant lives—public schools, thrift store clothes, no vacations —but we never worried about food. At the worst times, he would bring food home from his shifts as a cook. At the best times, a surprise royalty check would come in for one of his songs and then there would be steak on the table, a simple *au poivre,* bloody red, so we could taste it.

But it had been a hungry year. Until my mother started throwing these parties. She was doing her best. The guilt stirs in my stomach. Maybe I *could* help a little bit. I start washing the dishes.

While I scrub the pots, the men wander in and out of the room, taking their shot at me.

Isn't it past your bedtime?

No hug for an old friend?

Do you need any help with that?

You're doing it all wrong.

"They're dishes," I say.

"You look tired," says one man, that man, that motherfucker, and I don't even turn toward him, why bother, he doesn't deserve my time. "Do you need a massage?" he says, and he doesn't wait for an answer, just comes up behind me and touches me. That's what this house is, what it has become. A place where faceless men sneak up on you and touch you. The best part of my mother's marriage is the worst part of my life.

And also there is that thing between his legs, that thing I am always feeling from these men, and he is pressing it up against me. "Give me a break," I say. "Your attitude stinks," the man says. Whiskey breath, the breath of a monster. I can feel his lame goatee on my neck. For the rest of my life I will date clean-shaven men. I elbow him and he catches my arm. His other arm against my wrist, pushing me up against the counter. "This is my house," I say. And I start to cry and it doesn't matter to him. Because this is what these men do. This is when they strike. When you're tired and you're young and you're over it and you've been putting up with other crap all night long and you're weak, you're fragile, and your mother is depressed and your father is dead and your brother lives downtown now and all you want to do is clean your house and go to bed.

Then suddenly there is another man telling him to stop, and there I am in a puddle on the floor, and there is my mother making alarmed noises in the other room—"Everybody out! Everybody out!"—and anyway it's the last party of its kind, although there are other parties to come in our home, graduation parties, birthday parties, baby showers, but none like this, no hazy parties ever again. Soon after the last one my mother gets a loan from her parents, whom she hates, *hates*, but these are the choices we have to make sometimes. A few months after that, a royalty check shows up for a song my father did for a 1960s television show, recently revived on basic cable. Then my mother's friend Betsy leaves her second husband and she gets more alimony than she knows what to do with. Finally my mother gets a new job, and we all throw up our hands in relief, hallelujah, because that means the most to her, that she's doing it herself.

I don't know about any of this then, though. While my mother kicks the last man out, I sneak off to my bedroom. There I cry and think about the blocks of cheese I have hidden in the crisper, and how I'm sure they will be the last nice things I will ever eat. And then there my mother is, next to me in bed, apologizing. She has done this before, tried to curl her flesh up next to mine, both as an apology and for her own comfort. There is not a person alive who doesn't want something from me, I think. There is no action uncalculated. Nothing is free. Nothing is pure.

"This is what I've been telling you," I say to her. "These

people are disgusting. These men are disgusting." "I didn't know," she says, and I look in her face to see if she is stupid or a liar and I can't tell and anyway I don't know which would be worse.

"Out," I say. "Get out. For god's sake let me sleep already."

There is no sleep of the innocent anymore, I think again as she shuts the door. I fold myself up into a ball and hold myself tightly. My own flesh, my own comfort, mine.

NINA

My coworker Nina has to give her first big presentation. She's been staying late for weeks working on it, and she's nervous about it, so I've stayed late a few nights too, helping her, because I feel for her, I know what it's like just starting out, and also I don't have a lot going on these days otherwise. On one of these nights she expresses her anxiety about her career, the sense that she'll be found out as an impostor. "I feel like I have this big secret, and the secret is that I don't know what I'm doing and it's only a matter of time before they find out," she says. I tell her she's as talented and qualified as anyone else. What I don't tell her is she probably can do better than this job and she should get out now. But actually it's a pretty good job for someone her age, it's just not a good job for someone my age, and maybe the conversation I should be having is with myself.

Our boss, Bryce, has been there too, a few evenings, and he's stopped by our cube and murmured vaguely supportive yet unhelpful things. Like: "You two. Look at you two. Working." And: "I'm impressed by your commitment to your work but don't stay too late. Remember: life-work balance." He has a small cottage in the Hamptons and a wife who works at another big agency and also a boat, and he has pictures of all of those things in his office, though not in the same frame. One night Bryce looks over our shoulders at the work in progress and makes Nina needlessly move a pixel. "Put it back," I say after he leaves. "I promise you he'll never notice." But she keeps it where it is.

The weekend before the presentation I have an awful conversation with a man I am seeing named Matthew. It is awful for myriad reasons. Then I go home and have an equally terrible phone conversation with my mother. Must every discussion end in tears? Must every meal? Must every breath? Right now, yes. I decide I need an extra day off, so on Monday I call in sick and smoke pot all day and order pizza and Diet Coke on Seamless and consume all of these things by myself, and when I'm done I go for a walk on the waterfront. I think about death on this walk, my own mortality and that of every person to whom I'm related. I stand on the end of a pier next to a construction site. This is how people used to do it a long time ago, just throw themselves off the edge of something, quietly, a lonely death, yet a romantic one, nearly heroic or at least bold, a big leap in the air into the distance, a powerful splash waiting for you, and then great gallons of water inside of you until you can no longer breathe, until you are sunk, your last thought perhaps: Will they miss me when I'm gone? But more likely, simply: *Oh.*

Only this isn't the ocean, this is the East River, and I wouldn't die this way, this far a leap is nothing, twenty feet perhaps, and death seems unavailable to me in that moment, and anyway I only wanted to consider it as a concept. So I go home instead, drink half a bottle of wine, masturbate, pass out, wake up the next morning, and go to work, because today is Nina's presentation and I can't wait to see how she does.

So here is what happens: she shows up for work in a tight dress made of lavender strips that appear to be bandaged around her body. How did you get that on? is a question I want to ask but do not. She looks amazing. She is pinkie-thin and the dress is flattering, but also a little sleazy. Like there's Nina, all of her, all the little mounds and curves of Nina, packaged in rayon. It is not office wear. It is Nina wear.

Also: full makeup, blowout, smells fantastic, diamond earrings, heels, everything.

I try to remember what I wore for my first presentation, and even though I can't, because it was more than a decade ago, I know it was nothing like that. I skew toward black, classic dark New York mystery—or is it apathy? Nina's a designer through and through. She understands the full package.

She is also twenty-six and has been on Instagram since college and knows about angles and looks and desires in a way I can never understand or care about, or at least care about anymore.

"You look nice," I say.

"This old thing," she says, and she barely smiles. All that glamour and she's still nervous. I love her for caring, I love her for trying.

"You got this, Nina," I say.

During her presentation it is hard not to stare at her as a physical object because she is young and lovely and there are all those mounds, too. I watch the eyes of everyone else in the room to see if they are paying attention to her flesh or her words. The only ones looking consistently at Nina are Bryce and me, and he's required to pay attention. If this presentation is for anyone, it's him. I've worked with him for a long time. He's good at maintaining focus, or at least appearing to. Everyone else is interested in their devices, looking up at her only on occasion. In my day, men would have given her all the male gaze available. I can't decide if this is progress or an insult.

I think about when I used to dress that way, not in that dress, obviously, but in that flesh. I will never do it again. I have learned all kinds of lessons from dressing that way, great lessons, terrible lessons, boring lessons, all of them, the big one being no matter how much you own yourself and your body and your mind, there are men who will al-

ways try to seek power over your body, even if it is just with
their eyes, although often it is with their words and sometimes with their hands.

Watching Nina, I feel like I am relearning all these lessons at once, a fluttering of images from my own life across
her flesh. I suck in a big, loud, anxious breath and everyone
looks at me. "Sorry," I say, and pluck a small ham sandwich
from the catering tray. Somebody had to take the first sandwich. Soon everyone else follows suit, and we are all eating
at once while Nina talks. Apologies, Nina.

Regardless of our conspicuous consumption, Nina does
an incredible job: she is smooth, well rehearsed, and thor-
oughly entrenched in the work. Bryce asks a question and
she answers it before he finishes his sentence. She's no vi-
sionary but she knows significantly more than anyone else
in the room about the thing she's discussing. I could not
compete. I am proud of her.

Later, at our desks, I high-five her and we both laugh.
"Let's get a drink later," I say. "Let's get a drink *now*," she
says. It is two p.m. Sitting in my inbox is an email from my
mother, apologizing for her behavior. I don't feel like reply-
ing to it, and so I don't. We both shut down our comput-
ers and discreetly leave the building. We go to a hotel bar
six blocks away, and I order a Manhattan and Nina orders
a gin martini, and we drink them very quickly and then
order another round, and before long we are destroyed.
Nina keeps checking her phone, which rewards her with

frequent messages; theirs is a true love. "Do you think anyone will notice we're gone?" she says. "They're going to
notice that dress is missing," I say. She laughs and says, "It's
pretty hot, right?" I finish my drink. I ask her why she wore
it. "Do you care that people were staring at your body? I
mean, I was staring at it. It was all there for me to look at."

"I don't care if anyone sexualizes me as long as they remember me," she says. "I don't trust anyone anyway." "I
don't either," I say. We drink more. We begin to tell each
other our secrets, about the things men have done to us,
the horrible things. Since I am older, I have had more time
to have had horrible things happen to me, but she has the
extra layer of being Korean, and there's a fetishization that
goes along with being of Asian descent in this country that I,
average Jewess, have never had to contend with. She shares
some stories with me: creepy high school teachers, creepy
college professors, creepy creeps. "No one's ever followed
me on the subway like that before," I admit. "Like once a
week it happens," she says. She checks her phone again and
sighs. Her real desires remain unfulfilled.

I tell her about the men who came through my household after my father died. My mother was always inviting
over all these pothead social activists. A few of them would
insist I sit on their lap and I could feel them hard up against
me. "That was how I got attention, whether I wanted it or
not," I say. "It was always a secret between me and them."

"Did they ever stick it in?" she asks. "I always wore pants to dinner at my house," I say.

One more drink and we're sharing our rape stories. Nearly every woman I know has one. If I had a nickel for every time I've heard one of these stories I could buy an enormous, plush pillow with which to smother my tear-stained face. Near rape, date rape, rape rape, it's all the same, I think. Close enough is rape. Once I had a friend tell me this breathless, elaborate story about fighting off a drunk man at a party. He tears her dress, scratches her skin, throttles her throat, and it ends with her punching him in the eye, but, she points out repeatedly, *he never actually fucks her.* "Thank god nothing happened," she said to me. I stared at her, and then slowly responded. "Yes," I said. "Thank god for that."

Nina's phone vibrates and she looks at it, scrolls, sighs with annoyance, and says, "Whatever," and I say, "Exactly," and we clink glasses and I tell her one more time that she did a good job on her presentation and she says, "Are you sure?" and I say, "I am sure," and she says, "You wouldn't lie to me, right?" and I say, "Nina, I am not here to lie to you, I am here to be your friend," and she says, "Sister," and I say, "That's right, sister."

Three drinks in and it is five p.m. and the bar is starting to fill up. Nina spills a little of her cocktail on her dress. The liquid is clear and it doesn't matter, but it's upsetting to her nonetheless and she grabs her purse and crosses the bar dramatically and ends up walking into the kitchen and then a waiter turns her around and points her in the right direction. I watch all this chuckling to myself. Oh, Nina, I think, you and your tight little dress.

Then her phone buzzes in front of me and I look at it because I am pie-eyed and also because I want to know what's going on in her life that she's not telling me. It's a text from Bryce telling her he was glad she bought the dress after all, and then another text from him telling her how hot she looked in it, and then another text from him telling her that he would like to take it off her, and then another asking her to meet him at seven, and then a final text indicating specific oral desires, both given and received. And I say to myself: *Oh.* I don't need to jump off cliffs into oceans to die, because every day there is a little death waiting for me. All I have to do is wake up and walk out the front door.

Indigo Gets a Divorce

We meet in the courtyard of a café near her loft, sunlight dotting us through a makeshift roof of narrow wooden beams. Overhead also are lustrous grapevines, which are spotted with nascent green grapes as small as nipples. Indigo is too thin, a wisp, the succulent post-pregnancy blossom faded. She is wearing a long scarf of raw, gray, glittering silk, and a flowing black dress, crystals embedded along the chest and the base of the skirt. This is her version of mourning.

I say, "Tell me everything."

Her husband, Todd, has moved into a corporate apartment near his office. "Not that he was home that much to start," she says. "Poor little Efraim," I say. He is resting in a baby seat on the chair next to her. "He must miss his daddy." "You can't miss something that's already gone," she says. Her mother flew in from Trinidad the instant she heard and is cleaning their house as we sit there. "She fired the cleaning woman," says Indigo. "Now I'll never get rid of her." She takes a deep, meditative breath, and I wait for her to say something balanced or forgiving or restorative, and she says, "I can't believe I'll be stuck with my mother in my home for the next eighteen years."

"I didn't see any of this coming," I say. I would have called a totally different ending to their story. Divorce, perhaps, but ten years down the road, another child or two between them. We have expectations of our friends. I thought she was gone forever, off to Baby World, like all the other people in my life who've had children: Miriam, who moved to Connecticut with Howard and the twins, at last, Connecticut, a place to collapse; or Peter and Glenn, who moved to the DC suburbs for Glenn's job but also because it was a better place to raise their adopted Chinese baby, Cassandra; or Pam, sweet Pam, who moved nowhere at all, just stayed in the same old apartment in Astoria, but disappeared, withdrew, a soldier surrendering early in the war.

I had especially enjoyed seeing Indigo from a distance, as if she were a sunset in the rearview mirror after a long day's drive. I admired the beauty of her life, the bold colors of the sky that surrounded her. She always seemed rested and refreshed. There was a husband, a new husband who loved her. And she had such big windows in her apartment yet you could barely hear any noise from the street below.

I liked knowing it existed, that life, even if it didn't exist for me.

Tea arrives, and neither of us touches it.

They'd been married only a short time, two years. From the start Todd hadn't been there. His work hours hadn't slowed. Perhaps they had even increased. He worked on Wall Street, within walking distance of their Tribeca loft, and yet he always seemed to arrive home in a taxi. Where was he coming from? What had he been doing with his time? Before the baby she'd met him for dinner, they'd gone out on the town. Post-baby, she stayed home by herself. How had they slid into this separation? Didn't he love the child? Didn't he want to see the child? Did he even like the child? This was his child, look at this child, she had made this child for him, a representation of her love for him, a gift, a child, a gift. Ceaselessly offering the baby to him.

"Don't you like your baby?" she'd said.

"I like him fine," he'd said.

"It's me, then," she'd said.

"It's not you," he'd said. "But it's not *not* you either."

"Did you strike him where he stood?" I ask. "Did you stab him with a kitchen knife? I think you could have gotten away with it. I really think a jury would have been on your side."

"No, I was terrible, he was right," she says. "And I've never been this way before. Only I couldn't stand him ignoring Effy, because he is precious and small and a tiny jewel from the heavens and he needs love." She starts to unravel the glittering silk scarf from her neck. "I am comfortable in my own space, you know? Here I am, you're here, we're all here on this planet, sharing the same space." She has her hands on either end of the scarf and she's doing this thing where she is wrapping the edges around her wrists and it looks like she's binding herself, there's something ritualistic going on, but it feels unfamiliar, invented just in the moment.

"Have you been doing your meditation?"

"That's what Todd always asks," she snaps. "Of course I'm meditating. I meditate like a motherfucker." She stops wrapping herself up, lets the scarf fall in her lap. "I thought if I lost the baby weight it would help. Todd has always admired my physical self." Indigo's hot yoga-teacher body. We had all admired it.

"You know that's not right," I say. "That's not what it is. It's never that, and anyway, even when you were pregnant you were still astonishing." It's true, she glowed, and she had seemed thin forever until just before the baby was due, she popped a delicious bump. It wasn't her body, it wasn't her form, it wasn't her concern for her child.

It was Todd. It was his fault. He was having an affair. "How did he have the time?" says Indigo. "It doesn't take that long to stick your dick in someone," I say. "Sometimes it's only a few seconds if you really want to get into it." She chokes on air. "Sorry," I say. "I shouldn't talk about your husband's dick like that." Indigo says it doesn't matter. His dick was his dick; talking about it wasn't going to change the fact that he was now putting it inside a marketing director in the cosmetics industry who abused lip liner and had graduated from Smith. "How hard did you Google her?" I say. "So hard," she says. "They met in Tunisia on one of his trips for his microfinancing project. She was there on vacation. I saw pictures of the two of them together. Holding cocktails." I gasp. "With fruit wedges," she says. "Disgusting," I say.

"I am trying to rise above." She looks toward the sky for guidance.

I had thought I would never have Indigo in my life again. I had seen her once since she had her baby and that was all I ever expected. And now I could take pleasure in her downfall but I do not. Because here she was: bitter and edgy, and more like me. "Whatever you need from me," I say. "Just ask." I had been this way forever, or for at least as long as I could remember. I would welcome her to the fold if that was what she needed to hear. "Your husband is a terrible man," I say. My Indigo who taught me nasal breathing exercises to cool the mind and insisted I was beautiful every time I saw her, her hands on my wrists, rubbing up my arms to my shoulders and neck. "Look at you," she would say. "Look at beautiful you."

I am always merely in the state of just knowing her, I realize now. I bear witness to her life while I am in the thick of my own misery and joy and wastefulness and excess. Her life is architected, elegant and angular, a beauty to behold, and mine is a stew, a juicy, sloppy mess of ingredients and feelings and emotions, too much salt and spice, too much anxiety, always a little dribbling down the front of my shirt. But have you tasted it? Have you tasted it. It's delicious.

Indigo's phone rings. "I have to take this; it's my lawyer." Before she leaves the courtyard, she hands me the baby without asking if I want him. This is, frankly, rude. So unlike my old Indigo. Here, hold this creature you don't even really know that well. But I take him, I allow him to play with my hair, I, uncontrollably, make kissy noises at him. I think of my niece in New Hampshire, the one who is dying, who has never been fully awake. I choke back a sob. Effy is scrumptious and adorable. Poor Sigrid never had a chance to show us her tricks. I bet she would have had some really good tricks. "Who couldn't love you, Effy? Who wouldn't want to spend every minute of their time with you?" He touches my face, my cheeks, my lips, my chin, and coos and laughs. "What kind of bastard would walk away from you, Effy?" He cocks his head. I hug Effy gently to me. I cannot resist.

Indigo appears at the table; her clothes, her breath awhirl, aglitter. "How rich are you going to be?" I ask. "I was already rich once I married him," she replies. "Now it's just a question of staying rich." And then she returns to her-

self, appalled by her own words. She pulls a breath from inside her depths, seeks and finds that elusive creature, her
center. "The money is for Effy, not me. If he can walk away
from Effy so easily now, who knows if he'll take care of
him down the road." She takes Effy back from me. Bye,
Effy, I hardly knew ye. "I don't care about the money. You
know I have never cared about the money, right?" I nod.
"I loved him. He was smart and successful and so handsome, wickedly handsome, and he spoiled me rotten, and
held my hand, and he made me come. All the things you
want a man to do, he did. He wasn't funny, though. I was
the funny one, can you believe it? I'm not even that funny,"
she says. "You're not," I agree. "I'm really not at all," she
says. "So think about how dull he is."

"You didn't want to spend the rest of your life with dull,"
I say. "But I did," she says. "I honestly did."

Finally we drink the tea, which is cold now, charmless
except for its burst of caffeine. Indigo pulls a small bottle
from her purse and squeezes a few drops of liquid into her
tea. "I'm doing a cleanse," she says. "I want all the toxins
out." "Me too," I say. "Give me some of that." She squeezes
a few more drops in my cup. We both sip.

There we sit, *cleansing*.

"How are you?" she says.

"I'm the same as always. Except now I'm forty."

"That seems impossible," she says.

"You can't stop time," I say.

I don't tell her about anything else that's happening in my life. Nothing about the dates I go on, nothing about how much I hate my job, how every day of work degrades my soul, how sad my brother seems on the phone lately, how I've been thinking about my dead father more than seems healthy, how much I miss my mother but nothing will ever bring her back to New York City. Those all seem like things I should tell her, but it's sort of nice not to have to think about my shit for a second, and also I don't want to wear her down. If I talk about these minor tragedies to her, then they will exist in yet another realm, the Indigo realm. And today is not about me. Today is about her.

Instead I tell her about some art I recently saw in a small gallery in Chelsea. The paintings were rough and beautiful. The colors were from nature. The man who made them was born and raised in Louisiana, and he lived on a farm with his family, and his subject matter was the nearby swamps. I read his artist's statement. It said that he floated on these swamps in a small motorboat every day at sunset for a year and that's what inspired him the most, more than anything else in this world. Not people, not politics, not war, not love, not money, not life or death. Just cypress trees and swamp water and peachy skies and the occasional threatening swish of an alligator tail.

I am shocked when she gasps suddenly. I ask her if she's OK, and she says, "That was just the first time in a long time

I went somewhere else in my head. I went away and I came back." "What about all your meditation?" I say. "It hasn't been working," she says. "I can't get out of my head. Do you know what it's like when you can't get out of your head?" I nod. "I've been stuck until right this moment." Her breathing calms. "It was so nice to go away for a while," she says. "Thank you." I hold her hand, and I think: This is a thing we could do for each other. Here, at last, is the way to make this work.

GIRL

2003, I move into an apartment, and I'm in my late twenties, and it's the first time I've lived in New York City on my own. First I lived with my mother and my father and my brother, and then just my mother and my father, and then just my mother, and when I went to Hunter I still lived with her, to save money. Now I feel like I can start all over again. Make new friends, construct a different life, set out in a new direction. We're in the same city, but the new apartment is far enough away from the old apartment to seem like a different place. Brooklyn versus the Upper West Side, a river separating the two homes. Every day I wake up and stretch my arms and feel two inches taller because surely I am more of an adult.

I befriend a neighbor, Kevin. He lives in the exact same

apartment as me but one floor up. He plays loud soul music early on Sunday mornings and the bass comes through my ceiling and wakes me up, and after a few weeks of this I go upstairs and knock on his door and ask him to turn it down. He's making blueberry pancakes and he's got running shorts on and his shirt is off and he looks pretty great half naked, not musclebound but just fit, tight, like his flesh is tailored to his bones. He apologizes, puts on a shirt, and offers me pancakes, and that's how we become friends.

We see each other mostly on Sundays. Sometimes he has me over for breakfast, sometimes in the afternoon I knock on his door and ask him what he's doing or I leave him a note that I just bought a bottle of wine and he should come down and join me right around sunset. I try not to make it sound romantic. I try to be his buddy. I am trying to have this thing with a man where I don't have sex with him and then fuck it up.

We have great conversations. He's a tax attorney, which sounds sort of boring but he's really good at it, he loves it, and he has big, important clients. He also has this vision of buying houses and renovating them and then flipping them, but he wants to do this in Philadelphia because he likes it there and he sees a better market for his purposes. This is not the kind of thing I ever think about but he makes it all seem interesting and it's exciting to be around someone who has actual hopes and dreams and a specific way to enact them.

We start to get closer. He is my Sunday-night whiskey and wine friend. I begin to count on seeing him. Sometimes we take walks along the waterfront. When he gets really drunk he tells me his favorite things about a woman. He loves the way they smell. He's all about pheromones. "I don't even care about perfume, although I like it. It's just that basic woman smell that comes off the skin. Ooh, it makes me crazy." But also he wears great cologne himself. If he likes the way a woman smells he wants to return the favor. Like: Thank you for smelling the way you do, I respect and admire it, so let me give you a gift back.

For a while I think I love him, or at least I *could* love him, but at some point he mentions he could never bring a white woman home to his mother, or more specifically, he could only bring a black woman home. He complains about his mother trying to fix him up, wanting him to go to church with her to meet a few girls, when Sundays were obviously made for morning runs and blueberry pancakes instead. But his singleness offends her. He tells me: "She said, 'You want a skinny black girl? You want a big black girl? What kind of black girl do you want?'" So I kind of forget about loving him because no matter how hard I work on myself, I'll always be a white girl, and a Jewish one at that.

And then he gets a girlfriend, this woman named Celeste who is just stunning, like model-pretty, creamy tan skin and six feet tall and thin, long legs. (The answer, it appears, is a skinny black girl.) I am impressed by how attractive she is. Like: Way to go, Kevin. I kind of want to high-five him. I definitely don't feel I can compete with the likes of Celeste. Like I'm fine, I look fine, I have big breasts and a tiny waist and good hips, round but narrow, and big fistfuls of curls, and well-manicured eyebrows, and rosy cheeks, and I wear all black, and I have a cool, smart look to me, angled and soft at the same time. I am not an extraordinary beauty, but I hold up medium well under scrutiny. I got my thing going on. But I always see them when they're coming in from their run, in their athletic gear, her hair in these adorable braids, one on either side, the two of them sweating and happy and in love, and I know deep in my heart I would absolutely never go running with him, so not only am I white but also I'm not fit in the slightest. It just would never work.

Celeste moves in and I don't see Kevin that much anymore. Then, a year later, Celeste moves out, and I start to see more of him again, but he's really hustling on the dating front, trying to get over her quickly, so some Sundays there are different women around, although to be fair, some Sundays there are different men around at my place, and Kevin and I start texting instead of knocking on each other's door because no one wants to interrupt anything. "Girl" is what he calls me. "Girl, where you at," on a Sunday afternoon. Sometimes he calls me that in person, too. It's buttery and slow, nearly southern, and I love it, because it makes me

feel feminine and doted on and I hunger for signs of affec-
tion in the universe, and I know it's a genuine term of en-
dearment. And I hate it a little bit too, because now I'm in
my thirties and I haven't been a girl in a long time, and even
when I was, I don't think I liked being called "girl" very
much. But eventually I decide I love it more than I hate it,
so I let it go.

One Sunday when we're at my place, at the small table
by the window, watching the sun set over the East River,
waiting for the lights of the Empire State Building to launch,
he tells me that he's leaving town. Some houses he was flipping in Philly need his attention, his office has a branch
there, the commute drains him. He needs a change. He
never got over Celeste. He's lived most of his life in New
York City. He gets tired of being a black man in this town.
He wonders what it would be like to be somewhere else.
He promises to keep in touch. I feel myself shutting down
to him. This is an act of betrayal: he was my first friend in
the building. But what was he supposed to do, be my neighbor forever? I have all of these thoughts at once and I utter
none of them out loud. I decide to continue to be his friend,
and this feels like a mature act on my part, and I congratu-
late myself silently. This all happens over the course of one
minute and he never knows how close he was to the two of
us not knowing each other anymore. "Philly's not that far,"
he says. "You could always come visit."

But I never do. New people move in and out of the building all the time. The neighborhood changes. Where it was once a scruffy industrial waterfront, now there are shops and condos and bike paths and European tourists asking for directions to where the cool things are, and I vaguely point and say, "That way," and it's not a lie but also maybe I don't know what's cool anymore. I'll be forty soon enough, or someday anyway. I read the internet, but then again, so does everyone else. I am distracted by the world around me and my family's issues and my lackluster career and how all the wheels keep spinning and I have never learned how to steer. I don't forget about Kevin, but I don't need to track him to Philadelphia. Weren't we only neighbors after all?

Still, he's in my life. "Girl, where you at," he texts me whenever he likes. And sometimes I am at work and sometimes I am walking out of yoga class and sometimes I am on a date and sometimes I am at a museum feeling nostalgic for my failed past as an artist and sometimes I am with a friend eating a big, delicious, expensive dinner and sometimes I am walking on the waterfront ducking European tourists asking directions and sometimes I am sitting on a park bench in the sunshine reading the paper and sometimes I am at home and it is a Sunday night and I am drinking a bottle of wine by myself, alone but not lonely, but definitely alone. And wherever I am, I text him back right away. Because I want him to know. Where I am at.

More time passes, we're older, we're still on our own. Celeste gets married and has a child, the internet tells me. A month after that, Kevin comes to town for a meeting and shows up at my house later that night. "Girl," he says when I open the door.

Girl.

He hands me some wine. It is an excellent bottle because Kevin has been doing extremely well for himself. I have also purchased an excellent bottle because I'm not doing too bad either, although he is way ahead of me in life. I can't say why things are different this time, but everything is a little more charged. Like he hugs me and he smells my neck. I don't even think it's deliberate. He's just a man who smells a woman.

We get to drinking, and it takes not very long for him to start talking about his search for a wife. He is still looking for a woman he can bring home to his mother, who has grown no less stringent about her tastes. But, he admits, he agrees with her.

"I'm not talking about anyone but me and my experiences here. When I think about who I want to spend the rest of my life with—my life—it's with someone with the same skin color as me, who's had the same experiences, knows why I'm crossing the street when I'm crossing the street, ducking my head, looking the other way or looking straight on—because she's doing it too. That's just what I want," he says. "For me."

"OK," I say.

"But I think you're great," he says.

"OK," I say.

"I just could never marry you," he says.

"No one asked me what I wanted, though," I say. If I wanted to get married, if I wanted a partner, nothing. Maybe I don't want to get married, maybe I have never once pictured myself in a wedding gown, not one single time in my entire life.

"All girls want it," he says.

That's not true, of course. I'm living proof, right in front of his eyes. But a funny thing happens when you tell a man that you don't want to get married: they don't believe you. They think you're lying to yourself or you're lying to them or you're trying to trick them in some way and you end up being made to feel worse just for telling the truth. But I don't want to agree with him. So I end up arguing the other point.

"I grew up here too," I say. "My father died and we had nothing. We struggled and it was hard."

"You grew up here, but you grew up white and on the Upper West Side, and I grew up black and in East New York."

"You grew up in Park Slope." I laugh.

"I grew up a little bit in East New York, long enough to never forget it, and I lived in Park Slope, and I went to college in Connecticut, and I went to law school in Manhattan, and even if I didn't live any of those places I am still a black man in America and the only person who could possibly understand what that is like is a black woman in America."

"Look," I say, but then I don't have anything to add.

"Your privilege is inherent," he says. "You will never understand."

"All right, I understand I will never understand," I say, and I'm not angry but I just want him to stop. Stop telling me about myself. Even though he is totally correct, both about me and him, and our personal truths.

"Your context is different than my context," he says.

"Fine, I know," I say.

"We will never be the same," he says.

He kisses me anyway and it's over-the-top spectacular because of all the talking and tension, but even if that hadn't happened and it was just a regular old kiss it would have been great, because our lips fit like a lock and key, click-click-click.

I push him away. I laugh at him. "That's fucked up," I say. "Get out of here."

"You're right, it is," he says. Hands up, submissive.

"I mean get out of this apartment. Really. I think you just should go." I am accustomed to having my feelings and intentions be discounted by the world, but not in my own home. That's intolerable.

"I'm sorry, I'm leaving," he says, and he does. But then he comes back five minutes later and he doesn't even say

anything, he just walks in and kisses me, and it is preposter-
ously good. All right, all right, take me, I think. Break the
impasse one way or another. And I hate to tell you something so obvious but we are all the same lying down. On
top of that, he and I are the same in our desires, which is to
say when he slips a hand around my neck and squeezes it
firmly while we look each other in the eyes it thrills me just
as it thrills him, and when I slip my hand around his cock
and squeeze it firmly while we look each other in the eyes
it thrills him just as it thrills me, and when we smell each
other and lick each other and push all of our parts together
inside and out and our eyes are now closed and we are just
feeling each other, we are the same, it is stupid how much
we are the same, it is foolishness, that's how it feels, and
then it starts to feel really stupid, that we were both fools,
because even though it feels fantastic, as soon as it is over, it
is doom. He does not stay the night. He doesn't even stay *the
hour*. He looks aghast, and I feel the same. "This was wrong,"
he says. "I don't do this anymore," he says. *But I do*, I think.

And that was the last time I saw him. No texts, nothing.
We let each other go. I don't know if it was worth it. I miss
him. But I was never going to be what he wanted, and he
was never going to be what I wanted. I was a girl but not his
girl. He was a man but he was not my man. In that way we
burned our love down.

GRETA

My sister-in-law comes to town for a meeting and asks me to have lunch with her. I haven't seen her in a year and a half, since I dropped my mother off with them in New Hampshire. It's not that I've been ignoring them; I call every Sunday. I just figured they were doing their thing, being this tight little family unit in the woods. Once they were all here, now they are all there, and I'm the one who got left behind.

We meet at Balthazar, Greta's suggestion. She used to go there all the time, boozy business lunches, hushed conversations at the bar post-work. I'd met her once or twice for the post-post-drink, witnessed the tail end of those meals, glittering media girls, their laughter tinkling like it was lined with crystals. An empty bottle of Sancerre in front of them. Introduced as her sister-in-law, assessed, and dismissed. Then

Greta had a baby. The baby was sick. Shortly thereafter the magazine collapsed. They moved to New Hampshire. They have Sancerre there but I'm not sure it tastes the same. I'll have to ask her.

Greta's late. The hostess seats me at a banquette beneath a wall of mirrors, artfully mismatched panels, unevenly glazed together. Above me, the tin ceiling painted a chalky white, fans stirring gracefully. There is a general ceaseless swell of noise. A waitress arrives. "I'm absolutely certain I need a glass of Sancerre," I tell her.

To my left sits an older man, bespoke suit, with gray hair like elegant snowdrifts. He's flipping through the *Wall Street Journal.* And to the right of me, against the window, there's a stylish couple. She's much younger than him, has thick brown hair, a freckled, petite nose, lean, golden skin, a silver necklace beneath a black silk shirt, a martini glass in front of her. He's in a pinstriped suit, dark-haired and glossy, Semitic, and is wearing an enormous, expensive watch. Together, they're hunched, hushed, miserable. There are no new friends to be made here.

Greta weaves her way through the restaurant. She is dressed as an impression of her old self. All black, head to toe. Long, fragile, dangling gold earrings that fall to her shoulders. Extremely high heels that seem like no fun to wear, but that woman does know how to wear them. She's put on a significant amount of weight, but she was so thin to begin with that she just looks like a normal human being now, with round thighs and hips and an ass and real breasts, with a little sag to them, and her hair is healthy, big, nearly animalistic. Her bangs, however, are a mess.

"Don't get up," she says, so I don't, and I start to blow her a kiss from across the table, but it turns out she wants the human contact anyway, and she leans awkwardly across the table to kiss my cheek and reach out for what could, at most, become a half embrace, and it turns out to be just a pat on the shoulder, because as she leans she knocks over my water, and it spills on the table and my lap, so I guess the physical interaction wasn't really worth it after all.

"I'm so sorry! I'm so, so, so sorry," she says. "It's nothing, it's water," I say as I dab myself with my napkin, and I feel this strange sort of victory, like whatever happens next I have already won lunch, or at least she has lost it. It's not that this meal is a competition, that's not what it is. I just need to feel like I have the upper hand.

A busboy comes and wipes up the table, and then a waitress slides a menu in front of Greta. "Get a drink," I tell Greta. "Immediately." She orders the same as me and then, without pause, a riveting, obviously delirious energy racing through her, launches in with the reason for her visit. "I've been doing contract work," she says. "It's boring, but it's money, and when you're working remotely you have to take what you can get." The wine arrives, and we beg off ordering. "We'll just need a minute to catch up," I say. Here we are, two family members, catching up.

"I guess my days doing interesting"—air quotes—"work are over. Is this part of being a grown-up? Taking what you can get?" I don't know what it means to be a grown-up. Or at least not her version of a grown-up. She's waiting for a response. "Oh that wasn't rhetorical?" I say. "You really want to know what I think?" She nods. "You're doing what you have to do," I say.

The waiter returns and we both glance at the menu.

"Get whatever you want. Get something good. It's on me." I don't know why I needed to say that. I'm certain there's something passive-aggressive going on here, but I can't get in touch with my feelings right now, or maybe I'm having several feelings at once and it's too noisy to hear the high notes.

"I should get a salad," she murmurs. "Why?" I say. "I don't know why," she says. "Get a burger," I say. "We're going to have burgers," I tell the waiter. "Cheeseburgers," she says. "Two cheeseburgers," I say. "And more wine in a minute." Greta drains her glass. "I mean more wine now," I say.

To the left of me, the rich man flips his paper, folds it in half, studies a chart closely on the page. To the right of me, the woman, her eye makeup smeary, pulls her hands away from the man. Her hands are smooth, pretty, empty of ornamentation, with a clear French-tip manicure. His hands, balled into fists, are thick. I look for a ring on his finger, I assume that's the other shoe to fall, but his hands are clean too.

"So I came to meet with them to see if, one, they want this to go long term and, two, if I can get them to pay me less, or differently anyway, at least this year." A long story follows about income caps for Medicaid and the challenges she and my brother have been having since her magazine shut down and she lost her healthcare, and how they live in fear all the time of, it sounds like, basically everything. Even though I talk to them every week on the phone, this has never been mentioned before, though I am aware of their struggle. I'm not an idiot. But usually we chitchat, we're casual. I try to make them laugh. I tell them stories from the big city. This information today from Greta is both worrisome and boring. Then she mentions that it's a good thing what little my brother earns is all under the table. That part makes us both laugh, her marrying a musician, her marrying for love.

More wine shows up. I text my boss and tell him I'm going to work at home for the rest of the day, and he texts me back, "You've been doing that a lot lately." And I nearly text him back, "So have you," but then I change it to "So has everyone else." Then I want to text him, "Come on, just do it, just fire me," like I am dying for his response to be "You know what, don't come in tomorrow," but instead he says, "True that," and disaster is averted, but I still have to go to work tomorrow so what did I really win?

More from Greta about Medicaid and the cost of medicine. Our food arrives and I think, This will be the moment when the subject changes. But it does not. I dig in, and I demolish everything. The burger is medium rare, and the cheddar and the patty and the bun are harmonious, a glee choir of a meal. Frites in mayonnaise. I cannot possibly have another glass of wine, though all I want is another glass of wine. But I have been working so hard lately at knowing when to say when. "We should have gotten a bottle," says Greta. "That would have made sense," I say.

I search for a lighter topic. I wanted her to have fun today. "How's New Hampshire?" I say. "Don't get me started on New Hampshire," she says. "OK, I won't," I say. "Too late," she says.

Gun racks, Trump lawn signs, and no bookstores. She has to get into a car and drive everywhere. She misses walking. This is why she's put on weight. There's no walking. She's in that house all day. She has to drive forty-five minutes to a movie theater, not that they can afford to go to the movies. They haven't made any friends. They're totally isolated. It's just her and the baby and her husband and her mother-in-law. In New York she had a million friends.

"It's pretty there, though," I say.

"Yes, you should see the sunsets," she says drily. "Maybe someday you'll actually come and visit and see a sunset."

Now I miss the Medicaid conversation.

The couple to the right starts holding hands again. Actually, he's gripping both of her hands with his. Gripping and stroking, and perhaps she's trying to free herself from him?

My phone vibrates, a text from my mother, inserting herself into the situation. "Are you two having fun?" "Mom wants to know if we're having fun," I tell Greta. "We're having a blast," says Greta. "Should I tell her we're drunk?" I say. "Sure," says Greta. "We're having fun and drinking wine," I text my mother. "Make sure she makes her train home," my mother texts back.

"How's that going?" I ask Greta. "Having Mom there." "I don't know what we'd do without her," she says with an elegant, heartbreaking poignancy. "We don't know how long Sigrid has left," Greta says. "I know," I say. "You haven't seen her in a while, I didn't know if you'd remember," she says, less heartbreaking, more aggressive this time. "How could I forget?" I say.

The waitress clears our plates. The man to my left places the newspaper, now finished, on the seat between us. He pulls a pen out of his interior pocket, and a small notebook. He opens the notebook but merely clicks the top of his pen thoughtfully, then repeatedly, then maddeningly. I had been on the fence about how I felt about him. There was a chance he was a class act, a genteel individual. But no pen clicker is a friend of mine.

"I'm still exhausted," she says. "By my life. But you know what? At least I'm not a boss anymore. I hated being a boss. Did you know when you're a boss you're never allowed to be in a bad mood? And you have to care about everyone else's problems? And I had a lot of amazing women

working for me, but women have so many problems, Andrea. The last year I was working, after Sigrid was born,
and your brother being his own kind of baby, and everyone
on my staff worried about the magazine collapsing on their
head, on top of all their other shit, I tell you it's a fucking
vacation right now to only have to worry about a terminally
ill child and how to pay for her medicine."

I'm technically listening to Greta, and I nod, I acknowledge her, but the couple to my right has turned into a real
thrill ride. He's holding a butter knife to his wrist (dumb, hilarious), and she's stage-whispering, "Do it, do it." Then he
pounds his hand on the table, and it's loud, and the glasses
shake and splash. Finally she begins to weep, and it's not
over the top, not an outright sob, it's just the sound of misery. The gentleman to my left watches this with amuse-
ment, a flicker of the eyes on the woman, up and down, is
she worth all the trouble she's causing, is any woman ever
worth this much trouble?

I am on Team Drunk Lady, obviously.

Her date does nothing. You stroke her hand, then you let
her cry, untouched, unloved, in public. You son of a bitch.
I'll love you, I think suddenly. I rise, squeeze between the
two tables, and pat the woman on her shoulder. Makeup
streaming, lashes fluttering, bloodshot lines threading her
eyes. I've wept in public before, like this, not in the daylight,
though, only at night, in a dark corner of a bar. "Do you
want to come with me to the restroom?" I say. She nods.

We walk through the restaurant, my hand on her back, guiding her gently through the tables, past the front entrance and a concerned hostess and the beautiful old bar with the wine bottles lining the walls, and downstairs, to the ladies' room, where neither one of us has to pee. I sit in the lounge while she washes her face, pats it with a towel, then puts on some lipstick. Her silk skirt is expertly fitted, and she's got a precise, sexy figure, tiny waist, big hips, slender shoulders: a structurally strong, shapely human being.

"I'm fine, honey," she says. "I know it looks like I'm not. He's just crazy, is all, like crazy obsessed in love with me, and this is what comes with that." She hoists herself up on the counter, crosses her legs, and pulls a cigarette out of her purse. Smoking indoors has been illegal in New York City for more than a decade. "You can't do that," I say. "Can't I," she says, and she lights it. Already I want to leave. I've chosen the wrong hill to die on. But I cannot go. Because she has a story to tell.

Her name is Dominique, and she is from Atlanta, and she hasn't lived there in five years, but since her parents still live there (she actually calls them "Mommy and Daddy" and it is not ironic; to her, that's just their names), she will always think of Atlanta as home. She won't be in New York forever, no matter what the man upstairs says, and by "man upstairs" she means the man she is having an affair with, not God, though she could see my confusion if I had any.

She was a summer intern at his consulting firm, one I probably would have heard of, she whispers, and I tell her that I don't know the names of any consulting firms because that's not really my deal, and she ignores me because she doesn't care what my deal is. This child. She was supposed to go home to her daddy's firm, which she might inherit someday if she feels like it, but he wouldn't let her, the man upstairs, and she's been here in New York for two years now. She stays with him when she feels like it, she goes when she pleases. He's too old for her. He's never met her parents. It's not their first fight and it won't be their last. "You two are a nightmare," I say. "You think?" she says. "All this time I thought I was living the dream." She lights another cigarette. The hostess enters the lounge, and I exit. "You can't smoke here," says the hostess. "Can't I," I hear Dominique say behind me.

Upstairs, I slide back into the banquette. The man to the left of me is now gone, his paper left behind, and the man to the right of me is on his phone, texting. Greta has the check, and now she's crying. "I've got it, don't worry," she says. "I'll pay it, just get me out of here." I grab it from her. "Greta, no. I'm not going to sit here and listen to you talk about how broke you are for an hour and then let you pay this bill." "Oh, *so sorry* I'm broke," she says. "Forgive me for feeding your family." "That's not my family," I say without thinking. "Andrea. It is," she says. I'm immediately mortified. I put my hands flat on the table and steady myself.

"Let's just both calm down here," I say. "OK," she says. The man to the right of me offers to pay our bill and we both snap at him, "Fuck off." He gets up and leaves.

"I was telling you about me and my problems and you walked off with a complete stranger," she says. "I'm sorry," I say. "Could you just stop pretending we don't exist?" she says. "You're the ones who left town," I say. "Because we had to," she says. "I didn't really know you needed me," I mumble. "Andrea, what do you think is going on in our lives? Can't you see what's happening?" she says. "It's all hands on deck." She's pissed, she's *furious*. "And—I can't speak for David because he's on his own planet half the time but I can certainly speak for myself—it hurts my feelings. Everything, *everything* we've been through together, you and me together, and you check out now?" "I call," I say. She snorts. "Your phone calls are appreciated but they are certainly not enough. We need you to show up." I say, "OK, well, I didn't think it mattered." "Of course it fucking matters," she says. "You matter to us. You matter to me." She takes my hands and squeezes them and her eyes are full of so many emotions and she forces me to accept them and I am momentarily winded by them all.

Across the room a waiter drops a glass and it shatters. A smattering of people applaud. They must be from out of town, I think. No real New Yorkers would clap for that.

Later I call an Uber to get Greta to Grand Central. It would be faster for her to take the subway, but I like the idea of her collapsing into the back seat of a car, being alone with her thoughts for a while, watching the city fly by her one last time, because who knows when she'll be back again? She grasps me as she leaves, kisses me hard on the cheek, tells me she loves me, that I'm her sister whether I like it or not. "That's not even a question," I say. "I've always loved you." "Then come for Thanksgiving," she says spontaneously. "Could you?" She steps into the car, blows me a kiss, tells me not to forget her when she's gone.

I always reel for a few days after I witness someone's personal truth. I walk around feeling like I'm wearing their essence like a tight sweater. With Greta, it's a wetsuit. It takes a week until I can finally peel her off me, but I wake up one morning, naked in my apartment, and it's all me again, and she's gone. No more Greta, I think. No more sick babies, no more sad brothers, no more lost mothers. They're there and I'm here. I'm free. And then I buy a train ticket up north for Thanksgiving, because I miss them all so goddamn much, and if I don't see them again soon, touch them, and talk to them, I'll never survive this life.

THE ACTRESS

An actress moves into my apartment building. I don't think it's permanent—her name is never added to the slot next to the buzzer—but it's an extended stay. She's famous enough that I recognized her face as someone I had seen on a screen once, but not famous enough that I could remember her name or the title of the film. However, I did remember the screen: Lincoln Square. I saw the movie my freshman year of high school with my entire family, a few months before my father died of a heroin overdose. He was asleep for most of the film. He snored and my mother tapped, then shoved, then hit him until he woke up. So it's no reflection on the quality of the actress's talent that I can't remember her performance. My father's was better, that's all.

She is light-dark-skinned, the actress, I think of Indian descent, but also French. She is eight years older than I am and looks at least a few years younger than I do. (Who can judge these things, really, but I choose to, so I shall, I will, I do.) Her eyes are honey-colored and almond-shaped, flecked with sunshine. Her hair is black and long and wavy, tangled, casual curls. She is relaxed in the summer, in long, flowy skirts and oversized straw hats, and in the fall she wears tiny moto jackets and tight black jeans and in the winter she wears long tailored wool coats from European designers. Always she is wearing great shoes.

The actress lives in an apartment on the top floor, one of the newly renovated ones, with a balcony and a view of the river and the city beyond. The permanent resident there is her lover, a German man with blond hair and thick sideburns and handsome lines etched into his face, a thousand stories to tell, all living in his skin. They hold hands in public, in the elevator, on the sidewalk, at the café second closest to our house, but never on the subway platform, because that's when they check their phones.

I'm basically obsessed with her. I recognize that "obsessed" is a word that's overused, but what would you call this:

- Every day I look in the mailroom to see if she's gotten any packages and where they're from. From that I've noticed the following:

- She's a shopper. She shops a lot. I would have pictured her twirling around in front of a mirror in a fancy boutique owned by a friend, giggling and drinking champagne, but she's just like the rest of us: not wanting to deal.
- Sometimes there are packages from her film agency. At some point during her stay I believe she switched agencies.
- Three packages hand-decorated by a child have arrived from Los Angeles. All of them are beach scenes, palm trees, the ocean, all the shades of blue available used to color in the waves. She was addressed as "Mrs." on those packages.

Also I have a Google alert on her name and I check her IMDb page frequently. And I follow her on Twitter, where she has only several thousand fans, and her tweets suggest she is not in charge of her account, some marketing firm is instead, which just tweets links to the latest news about her, which *I already know.* Still, I don't unfollow, because what if I miss something?

And I have trailed her on the street a few times. It was always by chance, at least initially: we both happened to exit the building at the same time and then ended up walking in the same direction, but then I kept going longer than I needed to, missing a turnoff

to the subway or the bridge or the ferry, just to see
where she'd land. Once she went to the juice place.
There were a few trips to the café. One time I think
she was just on a power walk, she kept going and
going. That was the time I was thirty minutes late to
work.

I mean this is either obsession in a basic way or maybe
just a high level of interest.

But what about this:

I casually mention to my coworker Nina, who is
twenty-six years old, that the actress has moved into
my building, and she says, "Isn't she old?" and I get
mad at Nina, even though I never tell her, and I don't
talk to her for two days, until she finally notices I'm
barely answering her questions and she asks me
if I'm mad at her and I say, "No, why would you
think that?" And then she brings me back a cookie
at lunch and I silently forgive her.

Is that some kind of love or something?
Or this:

I have figured out where she gets her fabulous
shoes from studying her packages and I buy a pair
that are the same as a pair she has, but obviously I

buy them in a different color, hers are brown and mine are black, and they are very expensive and I swallow when I click to purchase but I am sure it will be worth it, and then I wear them every day for a couple of weeks, sometimes just when I'm exiting and entering the building, and then I switch them when I get to work so I'm not wearing the same thing every day, and I do this in hopes that someday she will be wearing them too, and that also we'll be on the elevator at the same moment—all of this, clearly, pushing the boundaries of timing. But in fact it works, within three weeks of my buying the shoes, on a Friday, there she is, there I am, with our patent leather loafers, me riding up to the fifth floor, her riding up to the eleventh, and I point and say, "Look," and she looks, and I say, "Great minds think alike," and she nods, and nods some more, and then she says, "I almost got the black but I feel I have too much black already." She tilts her head, imagining her closet, I suppose. "Yes, too much black." And then it's my floor and I get off because I can't follow her all the way home. That would be too much. But I felt like more of a conversation was warranted than what we had. I mean: we had the same shoes.

Is it some kind of crush?
Or this:

I go to an art opening with Nina after work. I don't stay long, because it is one of those days where it is hard for me to look at art. Sometimes it is hard for me to look at art because so much art is terrible and I can tell it is a lie, that the artist is lying, and I begin to hate that art/artist for wasting my time. And sometimes it is hard for me to look at art because the art I am witnessing is good enough to set what I do with my day in relief, which is mostly worthless except that it makes me money, and so I am a bad artist in my own way. Tonight, the art is terrible. I down two glasses of wine, and then I drink another one while I'm waiting in line for the bathroom, and then I leave and I don't say goodbye to Nina, I just text her before I get on the subway, and by the time I get home she's texted back, "I left first."

When I get on the elevator in my apartment building, I hear a soft yet masculine voice ask me to please hold the door. It is the German man. I decide I am going to make him my friend even if the actress has no interest in me. It is a mostly innocent, slightly volatile gesture. In my head I think, I am just being friendly. He is wearing a denim shirt with the cuffs rolled up and black jeans and his hair is closer to gray than blond. I realize now that I am inspecting him and not her. His face: still handsome. I say hello and he says hello and asks me how my day was and I say, "Oh this city, you bob, you weave," and I pretend like I'm a boxer and punch the air and it makes him laugh. I ask him about his apartment. I tell him I've lived in the building a long time and I know they did a lot of work on the top floor and I'm curious how he finds it. I do not explain how I know he lives on the top floor and he doesn't question it. We are neighbors, I've seen him, he's seen me, I'm the girl who bobs and weaves: we are already nearly friends. He asks me if I'd like to see the apartment and I say, "Anytime," and he says, "Sure, why don't you come up now, then?" I can't think of a reason not to. There's nothing waiting for me at home but my refrigerator, my laptop, and death.

I take the elevator with him to the top floor. I wonder if she'll be there. I hold my breath while he opens the front door. Their apartment is spectacular. It is a rich person's apartment. A rich person with taste who also likes things minimal. There is a bare amount of furniture but everything looks expensive, the European patent leather loafer version of furniture. I look at the floors and the windows; that's supposed to be why I'm there. His floors are tiled, his windows are new, a sliding door opens onto the deck. In the bathroom there is a tub, whereas I have only an old, stained plastic stall. All the fixtures gleam. "It is very expensive to live here, but it is very expensive to live everywhere in this city. Not like Berlin," he sighs. "But what is?" I sigh in agreement. (I have never been to Berlin.) "So," he says. "You are here, I am here, what should we do?" "What do you mean?" I say. What *does* he mean? "Do you want a drink or something?" he says. "We are neighbors. We get to know each other now." But I realize I don't want to know anything about him. It is only her I am interested in. He is that thing on her arm. I have one drink with him anyway just to be polite and we stand on the deck and look out at the city and he puts his hand on my waist, like, lower waist, and I let him keep it there for a minute because that bitch wasn't nice enough about my shoes in the elevator.

Or maybe it's jealousy?
But what about this:

A few weeks later, it's raining. Summer rain, unexpected, but no sane person minds weather like that. The rain glitters down, hair in soft, damp curls, moist, sexy skin. I'm laughing as I run through it. It was a late night at work, a deadline I didn't care about, but I finished it, it's done, and I feel dizzy and giddy. I'll never have to think about that project again. Maybe it's the last time I'll ever have a project like that. I imagine myself quitting my job. I imagine myself with a new life. The surprise of the rain lets me picture a different future for myself.

Once I was pregnant, did I ever tell you that? It wasn't really a baby, it was just a few weeks old, barely formed, a concept, and then it was lifeless. I hadn't even known I was pregnant. I cannot tell you who the father was: it could have been one of three people. This was in my late twenties, still a slippery time in my life, more slippery than now. On occasion I cry when I remember this lost baby. It is not because I ever wanted a baby. Think of the complications, long term, short term, I didn't even know who the father was. That is not the kind of math I want to ever try to do. But I cry anyway because it was a path I could have taken and didn't. I cry for the lost idea, the lost concept. Sometimes I cry, too, for who I was as an artist and what my life could have been like if only I had kept going. I weep for my lost identities. I weep for my possibilities.

So that night I'm running in the rain and I'm giddy and happy and a little teary imagining another life for myself, one where I quit my job and I'm squeezing my brain so hard trying to figure out what's next, do I shut down my life for a year and just travel until I figure it out, do I move to the small town in New Hampshire where my family is and stay with them until my sick niece passes away, do I volunteer my time to help change the planet, do I stop being such a narcissist, do I find God, does God find me, do I sit quietly and feel the earth rotate and breathe deeply every morning until I am calm and happy and centered and capable of being *satisfied?*

And when I arrive home there she is, the actress, sitting on the front steps of the apartment building, a damp cigarette in her hand, her hair a mess all around her on her shoulders, streaming black eye makeup, cinematic as fuck. She is barefoot. She is not smiling, she is not enjoying this rain. She is trembling instead, not because she is cold but because she is devastated.

I walk past her and up the steps because we are at war, and also because her shame is not for me to consume. Then I think: This war is imaginary, and you have felt the exact same shame. I turn and walk back down the steps and face her, ask her if she's OK. "I don't know, are any of us OK?" she says. She uses air quotes. I laugh. She's terrible. She and her German boyfriend are awful. She is a terrible actress. But she's still beautiful, and I tell her that. I say, "I have always wanted to tell you, you're gorgeous." And you would think it wouldn't mean anything to her in the midst of whatever she's going through, because beauty can take you only so far and then you're crying in the rain like everyone else, but it still does, it's still important, her looks define her, and her face lights up, pleased to be recognized, pleased to be admired. I have made her feel better, and I am delighted.

So what is that, is that basically obsessed or high level of interest or platonic love or jealousy, or is it just humanity, me reaching out and wanting to connect with this woman, this actress, this person, make her feel seen, make her feel known?

I leave her and get on the elevator in the building. I am dripping everywhere, all of me melting. I want to be recognized too, I realize. I want someone to see me. What if I start making art again? What if I just did that? That is the thing I love, that is the thing I miss the most. For so long I have believed I could never catch up, but now I realize there's nothing to catch up to, there's only what I choose to make. There's still time, I think. I have so much time left.

ALL GROWN UP

1988, my mother is in the kitchen, on the phone
with her best friend Betsy, and I am in the living room
eavesdropping. I am thirteen years old but I am a city kid, so
I think I'm all grown up and deserve to know what's going
on in my house.

She's talking about my father, of course. He's a jazz musician—he can play any instrument, he's amazing—and a
part-time sous chef on the dinner shift, and his unpredict-
able schedule seems to be troubling my mother. "I can't
keep an eye on him all the time," she tells Betsy. "What
am I supposed to do, follow him?" He's been in and out of
the house a lot lately. One day he was supposed to walk
me to school but we all discovered at once that he hadn't
come home the night before and then my mother was late

to work and was teary-eyed and angry and held my hand too tightly and her eye makeup looked like shit and everything was a mess. "I have to work all day," she says. My mother has a job with an activist group. She is an organizer. The only thing she can't organize is my father. "Wherever he goes is where he goes." My brother has gone on tour with his own band and my mother is miserable and school is deadly except for my art classes and I am worried about my father. So I decide, all on my own, to follow my father. I will get to the bottom of this.

I wake up the next morning and dress in all black, secret spy style. My mother eyes me and asks if I'm depressed, and I say, "No, I'm just cool." I eat oatmeal, gather my books in my backpack, sling it over my shoulder. My father walks me to school, holding my hand, and we gingerly dodge the piles of garbage on the street. It's cold, but no snow yet, next week maybe. He's distracted, but he smiles at me, hugs me goodbye, tells me to be the best me I can be. I walk inside, hovering in the doorway. I watch him leave. No one at my crowded school notices or cares when I walk back outside. This seems normal. This feels right. I am keeping an eye on him. It's the most exciting thing I've ever done in my life. It is illicit and illegal and I could get in trouble for it. I love it.

He is wearing fluorescent-orange sunglasses, which he bought on St. Marks last summer along with three other pairs, one for me, one for my mother, one for my brother. I picked pink, my mother picked purple, and my brother picked black, because he really is cool. My father is also wearing headphones. He lights a cigarette. He's off in his own little world. The day is his until his dinner shift.

I follow him to the 86th Street station, stopping once as he gets a coffee to go from a street vendor. The subway platform is packed, the perfect place for a girl to hide and watch her father. We take the C train downtown. He's nodding his head slowly, he's smiling to himself. There's my father, happy, alone with his music. And this makes me happy, too. I like seeing him this way. But also because I feel like I'm learning a secret to life.

He gets off at West 4th, and so do I, following him to a townhouse on a small side street. He buzzes. He's in. I cruise by. I peer through the doorway. I keep walking. I anchor myself at the corner. I wait a half hour, and he doesn't come out. I wait another half hour. During this time I have an argument with myself about the pros and cons of buzzing the doorbell myself. I'll get in trouble for skipping school. Or what if I see something I don't want to see and then I can't *unsee* it? But what if my father is in trouble? What if I could help him? Also I am thirteen and my mind is impatient and curious and I am getting cold and I have to pee. I cross the street, and buzz.

I wait another five minutes, I buzz the door again. I hear someone yell, "Christ." Finally a man shuffles down the hallway in a bathrobe and striped silk pajamas. He is dusty-looking, pale, with an enormous frame, so he seems fat, or big anyway, but there's not a lot of meat on this man: he looks hungry. Yet he has these really great things about him, like he has a gorgeous head of cinnamon-colored hair, and also his eyes are the most perfect green eyes I have ever seen, the green seems to be crystallized, and he is holding me with them, I am his, I am in his eyes. Then he shields them from the white winter light behind me. "What do you want?" he says. "You selling Girl Scout cookies or something?" He rubs his stomach. "Actually, wow, I would absolutely eat some thin mints right now."

It is then that I recognize his voice: he is the costar of an animated movie trilogy I watched when I was a kid. He played a mischievous talking cat, the sidekick of a heroic talking dog. It was a very simple story: they had adventures all over the world. I don't know the actor's face as well as his voice because the rest of his movies are for adults, although I did see him on last year's Academy Awards show, which I watched with my family, a bowl of popcorn between us, and everyone got along that night, my father clear-eyed and present, my mother sated. He had clapped for this man when his name was announced and we all stared at my father and he said, "What? I love that movie." And now here he is. Standing right in front of me.

"I'm looking for my daddy," I say, slipping out of grown-up land. I say his name. "Is he here? I saw him come in here."

"Ah, crap," says the actor. "OK. All right. Crap." He peers

outside, looks in both directions. "Well, come in, don't stand out there." I step inside the house. Everything around me is glossy dark wood. "But stay here." He holds his index finger near my face, like I'm a dog. "Stay." He walks down the hallway into what looks like a kitchen in the distance and then moves to the left, out of view.

There is a bookshelf with framed pictures of the actor and other people, some of whom are famous. There is a picture of him on a boat with three other men, and they are all sunburned, and there is an ice bucket filled with champagne in front of them. There is a picture from another era, the 1940s maybe, and it is of a young, pretty, stern-looking woman, her hair in precise, upswept curls. There is a stuffed animal version of the cat character he played, with a cigarette burn in its eye. I float the idea of stealing something from this man, which has never occurred to me before in my life, but all bets are off, my mind is melting. I'm ready to both break and enforce every law that exists.

I hear a crash in the other room. Then I wonder: Why am I staying here? Just because he said I should? I listen to no one. I make my own rules. I walk down the hallway, into the kitchen, which is twice the size of my kitchen, and everything is new and shining and gleaming, and then I turn to the left and enter a side room where I see my father hunched over a shattered lamp. There's a television running, sound off, and jazz music playing. It's Ornette Coleman's *Free Jazz*.

I recognize the album because my father has schooled me on his favorites. He has the original album from when he was a kid, the one with Jackson Pollock's *The White Light* on the inside cover. A few months ago, after my art teacher contacted my parents and told them I had real talent and they should encourage me to apply to a magnet arts school, he made me listen to it. "To some people this album is perfect, and other people hate it. To me, it is perfect," he told me. Then he took me to MoMA and showed me the same Pollock painting in person. He said, "Our worlds intersect, Andrea." I love my father madly.

The actor is saying, "You know, this is really, like, ruining my day here, buddy. I just wanted to relax." On the low coffee table in front of them, there are needles and rubber tubes and a pile of little plastic bags. Just drugs everywhere, basically. I give a little gasp and they both turn.

"Honey," says my dad. He's still struggling with the lamp. "Just leave it, the housekeeper is coming tomorrow, it's fine," says the actor. "It's worthless and I hated it anyway." "What are you doing here?" says my father. "I followed you," I say. "I was worried about you." The two men both make an ugh sound.

The actor's voice turns kind. "We don't need this to turn into anything bad, not when you're such a nice kid, Andrea." He knows my name and this mostly thrills me. "Arthur, maybe it's best the two of you go now." "Of course," says my father. "Sorry to be such a bummer, man." The actor walks us out. "I have to go to the Coast tomorrow but I'll be back in a month or so. I'll check in with you then." "Yeah, be in touch." They embrace. The actor pats me on my head, then says, "It's not nice to spy on people, but I commend you on your sleuthing skills nonetheless." The door closes. The whole thing takes two minutes.

"All right, you," says my father unsteadily, slipping on his fluorescent sunglasses. "Let's get you back to school." Of course it's me leading him, though, as he shuffles along. He stops us on the corner, puts both hands on my shoulders as if he's about to say something, but really he's just resting. "Would coffee help?" I ask him. "It might," he says. "It'll warm us up, anyway." We buy coffee from a street vendor on West 4th Street, my father digging in his pocket for the exact change. We both take our coffee the same way, light and sweet. "I can't remember, is coffee bad for someone your age?" he says. His voice is dragging. "Will it stunt your growth?" "One cup won't kill me," I say.

And then somehow the coffee works. It doesn't sober him up entirely, that's not quite what it does. It speeds him up, though. All of a sudden he has *ideas*. We're on the platform, waiting for the train to take us back uptown, and he wants to tell me everything he knows at once. My father has wisdom to share. And I believe everything he says because it seems so urgent and important. He believes it, and he is my father, so it has to be true.

"Here's what they tell you, Andrea. They tell you that

you grow up, you get a job, you fall in love, you get married, you buy a home, you have children, you do all that, you get to be an adult. Like you want in this club? This is how you do it. This is it. This is the path."

We get on the train. Rush hour is over; we find a seat. We turn and face each other. He has gaps where he's lost a few teeth. My mother makes us brush and floss every night.

"Now that doesn't account for a lot of things. Like did you know you can fall in love with more than one person in your life? The boys are gonna be crazy for you, I can tell." He strokes my hair down to my shoulders. "Or you might not love anyone at all. You could just not love anyone and that would be fine, even though life is lonely and it might be easier if you do. But you can't be something you're not. You can't."

I'm nodding, but I don't know anything about love yet. Just Mom and Dad and my brother, that's love. Friends is love. *Love* love I don't know about.

"And did you know that most jobs are pure hell? And did you know that none of the rules work too well if you want to be any kind of artist? And did you know that it's easier to be an adult—their kind of adult—if you live a life of freedom, as in if you are a man and you live in the Western world or if you are a white person or if you're rich, all of those things can make your life easier, and all the opportunities are just sitting there, if you want them, you can

have them, and then you can be the person you're supposed to be. But if you're not white or if you're a woman or
if you're poor or you live in some terrible place, then you
could be fucked. This is why I love your mother, Andrea.
Because she fights to level the playing field."

His mention of my mother bursts the bubble we're lingering in together. Out there, outside of this speech and this
subway, the real world of our family exists.

"And also those things I just told you are completely fal-
lible, like your fucking life—excuse my language—could
collapse right before you at any moment. Like your children, your job, your love, all of it, could just go kaboom,
and then what do you do when a piece of your personal
puzzle disappears? How do you hold it all together?"

The subway stops between stations and the lights flicker
and go dark and he holds my hand and tells me it's fine,
we're fine.

"Not to mention, what about your own special secret
desires that thrill you like no other thing. Not to mention
pleasure. No one ever mentions pleasure. Why are we supposed to feel bad for wanting to feel good?"

The lights go back on, the subway starts rocking again.

"And worst of all, what if you don't know what you like
at all? What if nothing sticks? Then you spend half your
life wondering what it is you're supposed to be doing next.
What happens after that?"

86th Street. He walks me to school, signs me in at the front office, blames himself, makes the secretary laugh. He half-asses everything in his life so brilliantly.

He kisses me goodbye. "There's no point in telling your mother about this," he says, and it's true, and my whole life, I never do. What would be the point?

He's home that night and the next and for a few weeks after, and then he's gone again. My mother bitches about him one night, says some really harsh and cruel things about him right in front of me, and I start to cry. "I like Dad," I say. "Everyone likes your father," she says tiredly, "but he is a drug addict." "I know," I say. She kneels down next to me and holds me, but it is not for my sake, it is for hers.

Six months later the actor dies of an overdose. When we watch the Oscars that year, the actor's face flashes onscreen during the In Memoriam segment, and my father cries silently next to me on the couch. My mother says, "What on earth, Arthur?" and he says, "I really admired his work." The next day my father tries rehab for what I find out is the third time in his life. He does the work, he goes to the meetings. But then he relapses again, and this time it sticks, him and the drugs, and he dies in our living room, on his recliner, high, listening to a record. In my head I imagine it's *Free Jazz*, but my mother had turned the music off long before I got home, so I'll never know what it was, and now it seems too late to ask.

At my father's funeral my mother sits with her arms around my brother and me and sobs, "What am I going to do now?" She is sad and tired but at least it's over. I can feel her giving in to it; I hear the relief in her voice. Had she been waiting forever for this moment? To tip to the other side. Was she ready now, was it time, for whatever happens next?

Come Together

A book is published.

It is a book about death and dying and how to cope with losing a child who is born terminally ill. It is a memoir, written from the perspective of the mother, and it is something I would never read in a million years because it sounds super-depressing, even though it is relevant to my family and me.

My mother sends me a copy of this book with a note that says, "You should read this book. Everyone in this house has and it has seemed to help us all. I'm not telling you what to do with your life, but I think this might help you understand what's going on over here. See you at Thanksgiving."

I read the book. It is devastating. I sit in the laundry room of my apartment building reading it, waiting for the fluff cycle to end, wiping my eyes with the backs of my hands. There are at least three chapters that conclude with me sobbing. I am crying about this mother and her child and all the people around them who showed them love and also I am crying about my own family, the people I have lost in my life, my father, my friends, lovers, and also the years of my life that will never return to me. It is a singular head-crashing moment with mortality, this book. God bless this book.

I find myself posting a quote from it on my Facebook wall along with a picture of my niece, and I ask people to think good thoughts for her, which feels gross and overly personal and yet I cannot help myself, this is how I can reach out to the most people, this is how I can feel the least alone about this situation in this moment. I do not pay attention to the likes but I know they are there.

My coworker Nina sees me reading the book at lunch in our cube and says, "That looks like a bummer," and I say with a serious tone, "It is," and she smiles and starts to say something that I'm sure would have been witty and hilarious but then something comes over her, a cloud of wisdom perhaps, which is surprising given her age and self-involvedness, but maybe now is the time for change, and she catches herself and says, "Are you all right?" to me for probably the first time ever.

I call my sister-in-law, Greta, to talk about the book, but my brother, David, answers instead and we somehow completely avoid talking about it, and then he hands the phone to his wife and we almost instantly land on it, dead in its center. And I say, "Oh my god, that book, I might not ever recover," and she says, "Try living it."

I go out on a date with a man I meet on the internet and he has tepid blue eyes and is a smoker and his leg jogs a lot even while he's sitting and he works in IT and I ask him if he's read this book, and he says, "Why would I want to read it?" and I say, "I don't know, I just thought I'd ask. I was trying to find someone to talk to about it," and it's not his fault that he doesn't want to talk about it, but he really, really doesn't.

I call my therapist, whom I fired six months before, for a touch-up session. I sit down on her couch and hold up the book, and she says. "Andrea, I'm glad you're finally dealing with this," and even though she is totally right and I should have dealt with it a long time ago and it was a good choice to read this book, there is a smugness to her tone, reminding me of why I had ended the relationship in the first place, so now I've made two good decisions this year.

When I see my best friend Indigo for coffee, I tell her about the book and she says, "Oh, I know about it, all the mothers do, it's the book you read if you feel like never sleeping through the night again." Mothers, I think. She's in that club now, I sometimes forget. We've been working really hard at hanging out one-on-one ever since she and her husband split up. Her mother is more than happy to babysit for her. She continues: "I saw an interview with the author and I dedicated one of my yoga practices to the family, I sent my best intentions their way. It would be hard for me to read it with a happy, healthy baby at home. You almost feel guilty that something's not wrong with yours." Guilt, that's a feeling I recognize. "But do you want me to read it?" she asks. "Will it help you some way on your"— she puts her hands in prayer pose—"journey?" I throw my arms around her and hug her and tell her I love her and never to use the word "journey" around me again.

Just when I think I'm recovered from this book, my mother calls me. "Come now," she says. "Don't wait till Thanksgiving. It's time."

I ask my boss for a week off work. This has been going on for a long time, the days off, the early exits, the hangover mornings, the half-assedness of it all. I explain to him that my five-year-old niece has been taken off her feeding tube, and soon they'll remove her breathing tube. I don't bother to ask him if he's read the book.

"I'm sorry to hear that," he says. "You've had quite a . . . run lately. All the cycles of life."

"Indeed," I say.

"Well, listen," he says. "Do you want to talk about where you're at here when you get back in town?"

"Not really," I say. "But yes." I don't give a fuck. Fine. Good. Done.

I go to Penn Station and buy a train ticket to Portsmouth. Then I buy a box of Krispy Kremes, three chocolate

glazed, three chocolate glazed with sprinkles, three straw-
berry glazed, and three plain glazed. They're warm. I get on
the train and eat three of them, don't ask me to remember
which because I barely taste them. By the time I get to New
Hampshire I have eaten another three. I meet my mother
outside the train station, at her car. I say, "I brought you
something," and I open the box of donuts and she takes one
without even looking at it.

My mother and I drive deeper into New Hampshire.
I saw her at my fortieth birthday party last year and this
summer when she came into the city for her best friend's
funeral, and that's been it for a long time. We are quiet for
most of the drive, although she has a cough, a weird hack-
ing cough, and so our silence is punctuated with that sound
occasionally. I want to ask her if she'll come back to New
York now that she won't be needed to help with the baby
anymore, but it seems crass.

An hour later we pull up in front of their house, and before I open the car door my mother puts her hands on my
knee and says, "Wait, I just need to tell you something." I
say, "It's terrible in there, right?" She says, "Yes, that's true
also, but what I want you to know is Sigrid is fading fast.
The hospice nurse was here this morning and she thinks we
have just the rest of the day, maybe, to spend with her. So
be ready to say your goodbyes. Be there for them, yes, but
be there for her, because after this, you don't get to know
her anymore."

"I want to talk to David first," I say. "Just for a minute." My brother, sometimes lost to me. The thinnest of threads connects us now. A muffled voice, handing the phone to his wife. If I squint I can see the dying embers of our joint familial spirit.

I walk through the red door beneath the crumbling brick. In the house it's dim, and there are candles lit everywhere. There's a circular living room, and in the center of it sits Greta, holding her daughter. She never grew much, this little girl. I kiss her. I kiss Greta, push her lion's mane out of her face. Whoever she was five years ago, before this baby was born, that slick, urbane magazine editrix, has submitted to the behemoth of witnessing sickness in someone she loves. I squint for her embers too, her motorcycle jackets and French spike-heeled boots and vivid, inspiring confidence. I see yoga pants and heartbreak instead.

I embrace my brother, bald, slouching, exhausted, with a full beard, and I take his arm and walk him through the kitchen and out to the backyard, to the small shack where he keeps his recording equipment and instruments. I don't know what to say. Once, before his first band took off, we went to CBGB together, completely underage, bad, fun, kids, and we saw Sonic Youth, only they were billed as something else, a different name, Drunken Butterfly, and they didn't go on until last, like three in the morning, and we were so tired when we got there but we both kept punching each other in excitement, and then Sonic Youth went onstage finally, and played feedback for an hour and I was high off all the smoke and swigs of my brother's beer, and I felt like I was taking two steps to the right into a room I hadn't known existed before, and I was so glad I got there. He was the one who took me to that place. This person before me. This tired, sad man.

"I'm so glad you came," he says. He presses a button on his stereo and some beautiful and strange ribbons of guitar sounds begin to play. "I am so here for you," I say. "I am here however much you need me, or tell me to leave when you want me to leave. Whatever you want."

My brother says after thirty years of it, he's quit smoking pot. "I'm doing this thing where I live in the present tense," he says. "How does it feel?" I say. "Oh, terrible," he sings. "You don't have any left, though, do you?" I say. He shakes his head. "That's not the way it works," he says. He points to the speakers. "This is for her, what do you think?" A slow, dirge-like chorus kicks in, his voice layered in tracks. "I think she would love it," I say. We are silent until the song ends. "I've got a whole album's worth," he says. I experience a temporary moment of both jealousy and awe at my brother's musical talent, and his ability to tap in so freely to his creative self. But that's him, he won the family lottery, he got the best part of our father in him.

"Listen, Andrea, most of all I'm glad you're here so you can say goodbye to her," he says. "We've been doing it, I mean, I think it's done, we're done. But she's a part of you, too. I know you never saw it but the rest of us did, and it's important that you know that she was your family."

"I know it!" I say. "I showed up. I love her." It's the first time I've ever said those words, though. So I guess it was time to say it to her.

I go in the house, pass through the kitchen where the box of Krispy Kremes sits empty on the counter, back to the living room, and my sister-in-law stands and hands me the baby. My mother is in the kitchen and yells to me, asks me if I want anything. "Do you have any wine?" I say. "No," says my mother. I look at Greta and she shakes her head. "Is this a sober house now?" I say. "For the moment," says Greta. "I object," I say weakly. But I suppose it's all right to be present tense, as my brother said. This moment will never exist again, and this baby in my arms will disappear, too.

I sit in the chair with Sigrid. Her hair is dark, and soft, and it curls under her ears. She is thin, and her bones feel soft and tender, but angular at the joints, as if they were sharpened to a point. She is breathing quietly. I bend and put my lips to her head and I hold her up against me and I close my eyes and think: Your blood is my blood. You beautiful girl. OK, all right, good night, goodbye. Then I sit up and hold her small hand in mine.

Greta's balled up on the couch under a blanket, now, hair everywhere, monstrous, lush hair. Dark, dusty, brown velvet curtains hang behind her. I'll paint this someday, I promise myself. I must remember exactly how she looked

in case I never see this house again. I will paint her. I ask
her how she's doing, if she's taking care of herself. If she's
all there, if she'll survive this. I am thinking about her and
my brother, too, if their marriage is going to make it, but it's
not for me to ask, not now, anyway. Greta tells me a little
bit about why they made this decision, a few recent health
setbacks for Sigrid, a conversation with a doctor, another
conversation with a doctor, and then she says, "It actually
doesn't even matter anymore. This story is over." Shaking
her head, her weariness, both spiritual and physical, slow-
ing down even that simplest of motions. She takes her time
with this next sentence, but at last she says it: "I'm going to
miss you, Andrea, when I don't get to talk to you anymore."
"Don't say that," I say. "We'll talk." She gives me a useless
smile.

My brother walks through the doorway. I look at the
two of them as I hold this baby. Greta is watching me hold
her daughter, and she is weeping freely. He is on the other
side of the room, leaning on the small entrance that leads
to the study, hunched slightly in pain, his beard so wild it
seems nearly afloat. *Come together,* I think as I hold their dying
child. Now is when you come together, not drift apart. They
were the relationship I wanted all these years, or the relationship I thought I should want, the one that seemed closest to something I could achieve, if I ever actually decided
I wanted love. And they can't even bear to hold each other
up just when they might collapse. *Come together.* Forgive

yourself, I want to tell them. This is no one's fault, no one's failure. This is your success, even, for keeping her alive this long, for committing to this thing, this unknowable creature, breathing small puffs of air in my arms, a tiny train pulling into the station. I could never have done it. *I admire you. Don't give up on each other.* But no one moves. I think: I'm going to count to ten. And when I'm done counting, one of you will move toward the other, and that's how I'll know you're going to make it. I hold the sick baby's hand. It's nearly cold. She does not stir. I begin to count.

ACKNOWLEDGMENTS

Thanks to my early readers for their big brains & hearts: Lauren Groff, Courtney Sullivan, Bex Schwartz, Emily Flake, and Alex Chee.

Thanks to my people: Rosie Schaap, Stefan Block, Maris Kreizman, Rachel Fershleiser, Jenn Northington, Megan Lynch, Zach & Sarah Lazar, Jason Kim, Steve Toltz, Hannah Westland, Vannesa Shanks, and John McCormick.

A portion of this book was written at the Frontispiece Hudson Residency. Much gratitude to Colby Bird and Jacqui Robbins for their generosity.

Thanks to Brooklyn, New Orleans, bookstores, libraries, readers, and people on the internet, you know who you are.

Thanks to my perfect agent, Doug Stewart.

Thanks to my perfect editor, Helen Atsma.

With love, as always, to my family.

ABOUT THE AUTHOR

Jami Attenberg is the *New York Times* best-selling author of five novels, including *The Middlesteins* and *Saint Mazie*. She has contributed essays on sex, urban life, and food to the *New York Times Magazine*, the *Wall Street Journal*, the *Guardian*, and *Lenny Letter*, among other publications. She divides her time between Brooklyn and New Orleans.

READING GROUP GUIDE

QUESTIONS AND DISCUSSION POINTS

1. What does the Empire State Building symbolize for Andrea? Why does she compulsively draw it?

2. Andrea occasionally puts herself in potentially dangerous situations; one example of this is the encounter she has when she tries to sell her recliner on Craigslist. What does this say about Andrea, and what does the threat or suggestion of danger do for her?

3. Do you think Andrea is capable of happiness? How do you think she would define happiness?

4. How does Andrea use her sense of humor to create relationships with the world?

5. Andrea initially sees her mother's move to New Hampshire as a betrayal. Why does she feel entitled to her mother, and what finally allows her to let go?

6. When Andrea's therapist asks her who she is, she responds outwardly first, and then inwardly. If you were asked this question, what would your outward and inward responses be? Would they be different, like Andrea's?

7. How do you think Andrea's identity as an artist, or former artist, informs her personality?

8. Andrea hates her job, but it provides a steady paycheck and security. Do you think this is enough? Would you advise her to leave her job to pursue her passions, or is a sense of stability more important?

9. Why do you think Andrea's relationship with Matthew lasted longer than her other relationships? What was different about the power dynamic between them?

10. How is each character defined by his or her family? How does family contribute to or detract from each character's sense of self?

11. Why do you think Andrea is able to easily display compassion to friends and even strangers?

12. What sorts of emotions do you feel toward Andrea as you progress through the book? Which emotions prevail? Do you find yourself feeling pity, sympathy, anger, kinship, or a combination?

13. What does it mean to be "all grown up"? Do you think Andrea is all grown up? Do consider yourself all grown up?

14. Andrea doesn't have the standard milestones of adulthood—marriage, children, etc. What are some of her personal milestones?

15. How did the ending make you feel?

AUTHOR Q&A

You Can't Go Wrong with Heart:
The Millions Interviews Jami Attenberg
by Edan Lepucki

EDAN: *All Grown Up* is told in a series of vignettes about Andrea's life—there's one terrific, pithy chapter early on, for instance, called, simply, "Andrea," about how everyone keeps recommending the same book about being single. There are a few chapters about Andrea's friend Indigo: in one she gets married, in another she has a child, and so on. Some are about Andrea's dating life, and others focus on her family. I'm curious about how working within this structure affected your understanding of Andrea herself, seeing as she comes into focus story by story, but not in a traditional, chronological way. I also wonder what you want the reader to feel, seeing her from these various angles, some of which overlap, while others don't.

JAMI: I made a list—I wish I could find it now; it's in a notebook somewhere—of all these different parts of being an adult. For example: your relationship with your family, your career, your living situation, etc. And then I created story cycles around them, and often they were spread out over decades. As an example, what Andrea's apartment was like when she was growing up versus how she felt about her apartment as an adult in her late twenties versus her late thirties, and how those memories informed her feelings of safety and security and space. A sense of home is a universal topic. And then eventually more relevant, nuanced parts of a specifically female adulthood emerged as I wrote, and little cycles formed around those subjects. So the writing of this book in terms of structure was really an accrual of these cycles.

The goal was to tell the whole truth about this character, and why she had become the person she was—the adult she was, I guess—so that she could understand it/herself, and move on from it. The fact that it's not linear is true to the story of our lives. The moments that inform our personalities come at us at different times. If you were to make a "What Makes Me the Way I Am" top-ten list in order of importance, there's no way it would be in chronological order. And to me they're all connected. I hope readers see some of their own life challenges in Andrea, and if not in her, then in some of the other characters, even if they happen at different times. Everything keeps looping around again anyway. (We can't escape our pasts, we are doomed to repeat ourselves, we are our parents, etc.)

EDAN: In my mind, and likely in the minds of others, you lead an ideal "writer's life"—you're pretty prolific, for one, and you also don't teach. You now live in two places: New Orleans and New York City, which seems chic and badass to me. Plus, you have a dog with the perfect underbite! Can you talk a little about your day-to-day life as an artist, and what you think it's taken (besides, say, the stars aligning) to get there? Any advice for writers who want to be like you when they're all grown up?

JAMI: It took me a long time to figure out what would make me happy, and this existence seems to be it, for a while anyway. I'm forty-five now, and I started planning for this life a few years ago, but before then I had no vision except to keep writing, and that was going to be enough for me. Then, after my third winter stay in New Orleans, I realized I had truly fallen in love with the city. And then I had a dream, an actual adult goal. I had two cities I loved, and I wanted to be in both. So it has meant a lot to me to get to this place. I worked so hard to get here! I continue to work hard. No one hands it to you, I can tell you that much, unless you are born rich, which I was not, and even then that's just money, it's not exactly a career. And I think the career part, the getting to write and be published and be read part, is the most gratifying of all. Unless success is earned, it is not success at all.

My day-to-day life is wake, read, drink coffee, walk the dog, say hi to my neighbors, come home, be extremely quiet for hours, write, read, look at the Internet, eat, walk the dog, have a drink, freak out about the state of America, and have some dinner, maybe with friends. Soon I'll be on tour for two months, and that will be a whole different way of living, though still part of my professional life. But when I am writing, it is a quiet and simple existence in which I take my work seriously. I have no advice at all to anyone except to keep working as hard as you possibly can.

EDAN: I've always loved the sensuality of your writing. Whether the prose is describing eating, or having sex, or simply the varied textures of life in New York City, we are with your characters, inside their bodies. What is the process for you, in terms of inhabiting a character's physical experience? Does it happen on the sentence level, or as you enter the fictive dream, or what?

JAMI: Well thank you, Edan. I'm a former poet, for starters, so I'm always looking to up the language in a specific kind of way. I certainly close my eyes and try to be in the room with a character, and inside their flesh as well, I suppose. I write things to turn myself on. Even my bad sex scenes are in a strange way arousing to me, even if it's just because they make me laugh. It's all playtime for me.

All of this kind of thinking comes in the early stages, but also in my final edits of the second draft. Most of the lyricism of the work is done before I send the book out to my editor. Her notes to me address the nuts and bolts of plot and architecture, and often also emotions and character motivation. But the language, for the most part, she leaves to me.

EDAN: My favorite relationship in the novel is between Andrea and her mother. It's loving and comforting even though there are also real tensions and conflicts between them. Can you talk about creating a nuanced, and thus realistic, portrayal of a mother and daughter?

JAMI: It is also my favorite relationship! I could write the two of them forever. I am satisfied with the book as it stands but would still love to write a chapter where the two of them go to the Women's March together, and Andrea's mother knits her a pussy hat and Andrea doesn't want to wear it because she only ever wears black. I have pages and pages of dialogue between them that I never used but wrote anyway just because they were fun together, or fun for me, the author, but maybe not fun between the two of them.

Their relationship really comes from living in New York City for eighteen years and watching New York mothers and daughters together out in the world and just channeling that. These characters are very much a product of eavesdropping. I try to approach these kinds of family relationships like this: everyone is always wrong and everyone is always right. Like their patterns and emotions are already so ingrained that there's no way out of it except *through*, because no one will ever win. But also there is love. Always there is love. And that's how I know they'll make it to the other side.

EDAN: This novel has so many terrific female characters, who are at once immediately recognizable (sort of like tropes of contemporary womanhood, if that makes sense) and also unique. Aside from Andrea and her mother, there is Andrea's sister-in-law, Greta, a once elegant and willowy magazine editor who is depleted (spiritually and otherwise) by her child's illness; Indigo, ethereal yoga teacher turned rich wife and mother, and then divorcée and single mother; the actress with the great shoes who moves into Andrea's building; Andrea's younger and (seemingly?) self-possessed coworker Nina. They're all magnetic—and they also all fail to hold on to that magnetism. Their cool grace, at least in Andrea's eyes, is tarnished, often by the burdens of life itself. Did you set out to have these women orbiting Andrea, contrasting her, sometimes echoing her, or was there another motivation in mind?

JAMI: These women were all there from the beginning—all of them. I had to grow them and inform them, but there were no surprise appearances. I never thought, *Oh, where did she come from?* They were all just real women living and working in today's New York City, and also they were real women who lived inside of me. I needed each of these women to be in the book or it wouldn't have been complete. And also I certainly needed them to question Andrea. For example, her sister-in-law in particular sometimes acts as a stand-in for what I imagine the reader must be thinking, while her mother acts as a stand-in for me, both of them interrogating Andrea at various times.

And also, always, always, always in my work the female characters are going to be the most interesting. Most of the chapters are named after women. I had no doubt in my mind that I wanted a collective female energy to buoy this book. We're always steering the fucking ship, whether it's acknowledged or not.

EDAN: Were there any models for this book in terms of voice, structure, tone of subject? Are there in general any authors and novels that are "fairy godmothers" for you and your writing?

JAMI: Each book is different, I have a different reading list, but Grace Paley is my mothership no matter what, because of her originality, grasp of voice and dialect, and incredible heart and compassion.

As I began writing *All Grown Up*, I was reading Patti Smith's *M Train* and Maggie Nelson's *The Argonauts,* and when I was halfway done with the book I started reading Eileen Myles's *Chelsea Girls*. I was not terribly interested in fiction for the most part. I wanted this book to feel memoiristic—not like an actual memoir that one writes and tries to put in neat little box, perfect essays or chapters, but just genuinely like this woman was telling you every single goddamn, messy thing you needed to know about her life.

Those three books all feel like unique takes on the memoir. Patti Smith just talks about whatever the fuck she wants to talk about, and Maggie Nelson writes in those short, meticulous, highly structured bursts, where you genuinely feel like she is making her case, and in *Chelsea Girls* Eileen has this dreamy, meandering quality, although she knows exactly what she's doing: she's scooping you up and putting you in her pocket and taking you with her wherever she wants to go. So all of those books somehow connected together for me while I was establishing the feel of this book.

And when I was finishing, I read Naomi Jackson's gorgeous debut, *The Star Side of Bird Hill,* which is also about family and a collection of strong women and coming of age, although the people growing up in her book are much younger than my narrator. But it was just stunning, and it made me cry, and the emotions felt so real and true. So I think reading her was an excellent inspiration as I wrote those final pages. Like you can't go wrong with heart.

EDAN: Since this is *The Millions,* I must ask you: What was the last great book you read?

JAMI: I just judged the PEN/Bingham contest, and all of the books on our shortlist were wonderful: *Insurrections* by Rion Amilcar Scott, *We Show What We Have Learned* by Clare Beams, *The Mothers* by Brit Bennett, *Homegoing* by Yaa Gyasi, and *Hurt People* by Cote Smith.

This conversation first appeared on the website The Millions *in March 2017.*